My Clavicle
And Other Massive Mis-alignments

Marta Sanz

Translated from Spanish by Katie King

THE UNNAMED PRESS
LOS ANGELES, CA

AN UNNAMED PRESS BOOK

Copyright © 2025 by Marta Sanz
Translation copyright © 2025 Katie King

All rights reserved, including the right to reproduce this book or portions thereof in any form whatsoever. Permissions inquiries may be directed to info@unnamedpress.com

Published in North America by the Unnamed Press.

www.unnamedpress.com

Unnamed Press, and the colophon, are registered trademarks of Unnamed Media LLC.

Hardcover ISBN: 978-1-961884-50-2
EBook ISBN: 978-1-961884-45-8
LCCN: 2025938181

Cover photograph from Ulas & Merve/Stocksy
Cover design and typeset by Jaya Nicely

This publication is supported in part by a grant from Acción Cultural Española (AC/E)

Manufactured in the United States of America by Sheridan

Distributed by Publishers Group West

First Edition

For Jorge, for our fractures and our resurrections

"You must be tenacious. You can't write without physical strength."
—Marguerite Duras

clav·i·cle
: a bone . . . from Latin, diminutive of Latin *clavis*; akin to Greek *kleid-*, *kleis* *key*
—*Merriam-Webster*

key
: something that gives an explanation or identification or provides a solution
—*Merriam-Webster*

My Clavicle

I'm going to tell you what happened to me and what didn't. The possibility that nothing happened at all is what's giving me the shakes.

When does the pain begin? The first symptom? Maybe as I was jetting across the Atlantic to San Juan de Puerto Rico. Sounds like an exotic opening line, right? Though more like something written by a bestselling historical romance novelist than by yours truly. In any case, it happens like this: as I'm flying over the ocean through relentless daylight, I start to note the presence of a particular rib underneath my left breast. And, on that rib, I feel a bump like the head of a pin, or a little bloodsucking tick, and suddenly I'm sure it's the harbinger of a malignancy. Or a fracture in my bones. A reflection of my internal chaos.

I'm reading a book—I'm always reading something—that distracts me from the noise of my body, which clamors, shouts, calls to me. I'm tired of listening to it. For a few moments I'm convinced that this is it, there's no turning back, and this trip is the tipping point that leads to the end. Almost as quickly I'm convinced it's nothing, with an equal certainty, which seconds before had left my mouth dry, I was definitely going to die. The human body is bursting with apparent warning signs that turn out to be nothing more than farcical gags. Natural whoopee cushions. I remember my aunt Alicia who once went to the emergency room convinced that she was having a heart attack when actually it was just an attack of the farts. I grin to myself. I carry on reading my book, and as always when you read, you start to think of other things, and maybe that's the beauty of reading. Parallel thinking. Three-dimensional musing. Geometric shapes hidden inside snowflakes.

It's Lillian Hellman's memoir. An excellent book that manages to distract my brain from the steady thrum of pain, getting sharper, undeniable; it's not my imagination. Lillian is describing Dashiell Hammett's cancer symptoms. He doesn't feel pain in the middle of his chest, but his arms hurt . . . and one of his ribs. And he has trouble breathing. Lilly, I love you, but you're such a bitch for writing that, because now I am also struggling to breathe in the cabin of this airplane carrying me across the Atlantic en route to San Juan, Puerto Rico. Suddenly, I'm again absolutely certain, zero possibility of error, that I'm going to die before my time. I gulp a deep breath of the airplane-encapsulated oxygen. Not the highest-quality oxygen, but it calms me. And I start to wonder whether this pain hardening inside me like a bit of concrete is real or contrived.

Where does this fear come from? I'm normally an extremely rational beast, so I reject, perhaps too quickly or too optimistically, the idea that I've developed a fear of flying and I start to consider two morbid possibilities. One, which I've already mentioned, is that I really *am* dying, and this flight is the beginning of the end. The other possibility is that while I may not be dying at this exact moment and I maybe—maybe?—won't have to confront the problem for years to come, this experience nevertheless will start to wear me down. It will consume me from the inside like a flesh-eating disease.

Gazing into a mole on my body, I can see all of creation. From the first single-cell organism to the fish that developed lungs and legs to crawl out of the muck, I observe the multiple intermediary steps of evolution in my mole, following the rise of the vertebrates from reptile to bird to mammal. On the other hand, in that itching, mutating mole on my body I can also see, as if I were gazing into a crystal ball, the reality of all that oppresses me, the alpha, gamma, and beta rays radiating from portable modems and invisible but ubiquitous Wi-Fi networks that penetrate walls and pierce my body. It happens. To me and to everyone.

MY CLAVICLE

I practice palmistry on myself, and when I read the burn-scarred palm of my left hand, I detect a lifeline that, instead of just ending, branches out into islands and scalene triangles. Irregular boxes. I'd say that my lifeline starts to get disrupted at fifty years of age. This is my divinatory calculus, my prophecy, and it pinpoints the moment in time when my physical comfort and my publicized sense of well-being disappear. When the age of mysterious ailments begins. The fear of ending up a widow. An orphan. Or broke.

And then one day, not long after returning from Puerto Rico, I burst into tears at home in the TV room. The TV room is actually the best place in the house to do that. I completely lose it. I can't remain silent against this pain that continues to afflict me, radiating from the bump on my rib into my arms like the sting of a jellyfish. I can't keep it to myself, stoically clamping my teeth down on an imaginary stick like a snakebite victim in an old western who's about to have his leg amputated. I have to share my pain and my fear in order to expel them. Or maybe I'm wrong, and all these tears are just a way for me to amplify the pain and make it seem more real. Solidify it. Put it on a pedestal. In any case, I can't stop myself and I bawl fat tears. Moaning, congested, I hear myself and shudder at the howl in my voice that I barely recognize. As if it weren't coming out of my own mouth. But it is there, inside me. In my cave. Next to me on the sofa, my husband is nervous and in a quandary: Should he gently comfort me or brusquely stand and flee to another room to let me calm down on my own? I emit profoundly pathetic sounds that break his heart. He doesn't know what's wrong. "Cry as much as you like," he reassures me, then tries to get me to stop: "It's okay, it's okay."

My lament is umbilical, born from the origins of life, the age of dinosaurs. I'm trembling, and I notice how the contractions of my sobs make me feel thinner. My husband is getting upset: "What is wrong with you?" I'm sputtering and stuttering like a patient in need of speech therapy, until I finally manage to spit it out: "I'm going to die." He gently holds my diminished little face, my baggy-eyed, dark-circled little monkey face, in his hands. "I'm going to die." His brow furrows, and I clarify: "Now. Right away. Soon." My husband tries to smile and asks, "Why do you say that?" He knows better than to downplay my anguish, because if he does, I'll stop crying, go rigid, and erupt into a fury. I would like to help him. But I don't. Instead, I curl up into a ball, feeling the burn of my own body heat, which in the midst of my tantrum is almost like a fever. "I have a pain. And it's going to kill me." I say this with the absolute certainty that accompanied my funereal thoughts on the plane. Although to be honest, for five or six years now my thoughts have been getting darker and darker through nights of insomnia, constant pangs of pain in my joints, and increasingly suspicious gurgles emerging from my viscera. So my verdict is based on constant observation. I'm not just saying this.

My husband strokes my head. "No, no . . ." He tries to soothe me. "Let's go to the doctor. You'll see, it'll turn out to be nothing." Deeply immersed in my tantrum, I'm defiant: "I don't want to go to the doctor." My husband's concern turns to anger, and because he's angry, I sob even harder and I contemplate him with an expression of infinite reproach that says, *You don't understand me.* And then I retreat, a trembling mess. My husband's angry only because he feels helpless. "Tomorrow I'll call to make an appointment." I'm terrified, certain that my doctor will realize, without even referring me to a specialist, that I am going to die. My mysterious ailment, the small bump on my rib, the little tick the size of a pinhead, will turn out to be something obvious and incurable. I'll be betrayed by the pigment of my skin or a scab at the back of my eye that my doctor will read like a map of my evasive malady. My skin will release a pathological odor from the insides of my elbows and from behind my ears.

"I'm scared," I tell my husband, but I'm also so exhausted that I don't resist his plan to call the doctor. I leave it all in his hands, as if he could save me from something that neither of us understands. He believes me when I say I'm going to die, but he doesn't want to. He knows that to help me, he can't believe me. But then he has doubts and falls apart, relatively, at the thought that I might leave him on his own. If I weren't around, he'd forget to bathe, or to have coffee with breakfast, or to have breakfast at all. He'd be abandoned. He'd stop paying the electricity bill. Or maybe all these morbid death fantasies are just me trying to call attention to myself. Maybe I'm the drama queen here. Normally my husband's the emotional one, petrified by the idea that one of my trips might be a one-way ticket. He always picks me up at the train station where I always come back to him. I look into his crystalline eyes. I love them. I whimper, "I'm going to die, and I won't be able to enjoy all the wonderful things that are happening to me. I'm going to die and make all of you suffer. I'm going to die without being able to enjoy my happiness. I'm going to die when I don't want to die." As I speak, my malady, which is the same thing as my malice, starts to jab at my insides. I really need to shut up. My words are wounding me, perhaps irreparably. My husband looks at me, perplexed. But then he grasps my head in his hands, kisses me, and says, "No, no, no." He does exactly what I need him to do. He's there. He doesn't say I'm full of shit. He doesn't insult me. He puts up with me. I know he will put up with me forever. This knowledge both strengthens me and devastates me, as I take stock of my love for him, and of my own perversity.

Good health consists of eating yogurt, exercising, and regular spa retreats. I try to be healthy, but not a day goes by that I don't experience some new variation of pain: this tick stalking my chest, these spasms along my ribs. But also the unsettling sting of a hangnail, an inner tremor near my navel, a hemorrhoidal flare, wisdom teeth breaking through my gums. And my bronchial tubes, with their mysteriously labored breathing. I resist all these corporal infamies with the usual Christian resignation. Under these circumstances, it's a wonder that I can still be so very *charming*—and enjoy a loving relationship and an active social life.

MY CLAVICLE

Turning on my computer, I see in my inbox six or seven job offers for my husband, an unemployed fifty-six-year-old who no longer gets benefits. Mostly, they're jobs that don't make the cut: contract janitor, hourly laborer, truck driver proficient in Senegalese languages, dog trainer, industrial furniture repairman, salesclerk with a good appearance for four hours a week... "Anything for me?" my husband sings out from behind his newspaper. This is our world. That other world—the one with cell phone apps, online banking, and freedom from standing in line to buy theater tickets—makes us feel prematurely old.

Today, I submitted his résumé to a production company calling for men of a certain age to act in TV commercials. He'd be perfect in the role of the dynamic grandfather, the guy who uses Grecian 2000 hair dye or suffers from constipation. Although in the real world, that particular affliction is mostly suffered by clogged-up, menopausal women who aren't able to shit in unfamiliar toilets when they travel and require micro enemas to finally relax the rigid grimace of their mouths, not to mention their hermetically sealed buttholes. Our asses are lockboxes. Men, meanwhile, squeeze off logs as long as skyscrapers are tall. Their issue is diarrhea, for which manufacturers happily create products that ensure their intestinal issues don't interfere with their ability to hit on women, or snag a C-suite promotion, or catch a holiday flight to a seductive tropical island. In general, it's important to take into account the quality and consistency of shit to get an accurate diagnosis of any illness. The abundance of colon and rectal cancer—these days there's a lot of information available about all these issues—is lending prestige to the practice of proctology. I'm happy for the proctologists. In an ad, my husband could be the doctor who recommends eating yogurt. He'd also be great in the part of a mature man who drinks Actimel probiotics every morning so he can go out and do whatever dickhead things he does in the rain without the risk of catching a cold. My husband would also ace the role of the paterfamilias in a household that loves pizza. I hope they call him.

MY CLAVICLE

My gynecologist is an experienced physician. She's also my friend, which is why we always turn to her first. Hers is the first medical opinion we seek out now, and I say "we" here because my husband's sick, too. Sick alongside me. Sick with me. He's losing weight. He doesn't sleep well. He's a very sensitive man.

In my gynecologist's office I feel intensely selfish because she just lost two sisters to actual cancer. Or maybe the better name for the monster is *true* cancer. Cancer is not relative or fictitious. It's true. Like the monster that hides beneath my bed and blows on my toes. Or the monster in my closet. Or the monster on the windowsill at night. Imaginary cancer is another type of cancer. It convenes other cancers. Constructs them. My gynecologist is convinced that I'll calm down if she places her stethoscope just below my sternum where I've pointed to the tick. Maybe she doesn't really know me at all. Or maybe she does and realizes that despite her reassurances, my sense of well-being will collapse in the minuscule amount of time it takes my mind to go blank and wonder what clouds smell like. I am never laid-back. She must already be fed up with me and with all this. I don't think yoga and meditation are helping her.

I tell her, "My arms hurt. My rib hurts. I smoke. I can't breathe." She shakes her head: "None of those are signs of lung cancer." Stories about cancer are one thing, and true cancer is another. The line between fiction and reality is a solid brick wall. Then she tells me the story of a male doctor who comes to her office occasionally worried that he has symptoms of breast cancer. The chances of a man developing breast cancer are less than 1 percent. This man arrives each time with sweat beading his face and his hands trembling. His tongue thickens describing his symptoms. My gynecologist listens to her colleague, and she must be especially skilled to be able to counter the arguments of another doctor who's familiar with symptomologies and pathologies far more intimately than I. I know about them only from novels. Alexandre Dumas's fictional Parisian courtesan and consumptive Marguerite Gautier, for example, and other sufferers of tuberculosis, leukemia, and multiple sclerosis. Heart disease in particular. Or fevers and yellow vision. Momentarily distracted by her story about the male doctor with breast cancer, my doctor regroups: "Smoking sucks." She listens to my chest again. "You have rhonchi." She asks me to take a deep breath. "Mucus." I concentrate on my breathing and fill my lungs as much as possible. I hear her say, "The day you really have lung cancer, you'll know it."

I think about my situation. About my convictions. About the love/hate relationship I've always had with my body. The simultaneous esteem and revulsion that when I was just four years old led me to develop an animal-like fear that I'd get a varicose vein on my calf or a detached retina if I tripped and fell. "Such a delicate flower," they would say when I was growing up. "So sensitive." "Always whining." Variations on the theme. My kind and willing gynecologist doesn't really know me in the least. And as stoic icing on the cake, she adds, "And if you do get cancer, no big deal. You'll just die. The way of the world."

We leave the building. My husband looks at me in the daylight, trying to read my thoughts. He doesn't need to. I'm trembling.

A few years ago I wrote a detective novel featuring a menopausal woman who looked like the French film star Simone Signoret. Now that I'm the one living through the Change, I realize my story was too literary. It wasn't stereotypical, but it did come across as contrived to be bookish and sophisticated. Or maybe the sophistication of the true metamorphosis exceeds the charm of any metaphor. I got ahead of myself when I imagined the hormonal life of my character Luz Arranz, to whom I affectionately gave my grandmother's surname. I should have waited to learn firsthand some of the important details of all this dryness that arrives so suddenly and cracks you. Even my eyes are dry, and I have to use eyedrops. Then again, maybe I did the right thing by describing menopause before actually experiencing it, because an excess of realism would have detracted from the appeal of the prose. But no, that would go against my aesthetic axioms. I subscribe to many axioms—and their opposites.

Luz Arranz, the divorced, middle-aged, menopausal character in my novel *Black, Black, Black*, records in her diary the number of cigarettes she smokes each day. She gobbles chocolate and misses her ovarian cramps, the flow of blood down her thighs. Red on white. But that's all literature and gongoristic sonnets, because, except in cases of hemorrhages or iron deficiency disorders, menstrual blood is easily absorbed by menstrual pads. In her diary, Luz describes the transformation of her anatomy, real but mostly the opposite of aesthetic: bloating, erosion, a clock that stops ticking, tides that stop running, seasons that arrive out of order: autumn, summer, spring, winter. Luz waits for her blood, but her blood doesn't return. Possibly she feels less seductive. She misses the way her husband used to look at her, a look that might be called love, or desire, or both at once. Luz doesn't learn to separate certain emotions. In this, Luz and I are possibly the same. I miss my husband's desire, but only so that I can reject it. He and I need to learn new habits—butterfly kisses; long, intimate embraces—and change the names of certain things. Every morning when I wake up, I'm glued to his body, pressing against his back as if I were clinging to a tree, terrified that I'll fall. I snuggle under his arm like a puppy. I don't want to move.

What I didn't realize is that menopause is not exclusively about a mutation that leaves you feeling less attractive. It's something much more intimate, something that's intimate and at the same time physical, that I would call "interior." The Change is something interior and explicit. It's not just a question of how you look: dry skin, gradual capillary poverty, spidery veins on the cheeks, bags under the eyes, grids of wrinkles like the netting on a fascinator. Yes, I've noticed all of it, and sometimes it bothers me. Sometimes I'm something of a walking horror show, the body of a handball player and a face with skin flaking off. The worst part is that menopause provokes a sense of vulnerability, which in turn makes you actually vulnerable. As if all the fibers in your rib cage tensed up and that constant tightening was keeping you from breathing. You don't sleep well, you don't defecate well, things don't smell the same, and food doesn't taste the same.

You start to step more carefully to avoid possible falls and fractures. My mother says, "*I* can't even stand myself." At night, I get cramps in my toes that are nothing like those former involuntary movements, during orgasm, when that other, younger foot used to tense, then stretch, and bend and grow with pleasure until it broke the glass slipper. Now I'm a porcelain teacup from the waist down. I brighten myself with bleach. I don't want to be touched. I don't masturbate.

Just don't feel like it anymore, even though I still suffer from a demanding need for love. I crave all the attention that a child bestows on a beloved plush toy. That kind of pampering. I don't fit the profile of the ageless woman of a certain age you see in the women's magazines. Of the mature but vigorous woman who trains athletically with lubricants and a vibrator, so her vagina doesn't slam shut like the cave of Ali Baba's forty thieves. I don't want to be influenced by these models or force myself to be permanently pert and always on. I claim other pleasures now after having had my fill of the old ones. I have no regrets. Nothing would embarrass me more than turning into a middle-aged cougar who embraces a neophyte with her bingo wings. Actually, flaccidity doesn't bother me. What bothers me are all the external forces of digital spam and glossy ads cajoling me to buy medicine to cure an endemic that I don't really experience as such.

What I want is for them to make the pain stop. To find its source. To extract the anguish from my heart and separate it somehow from the pain, in turn giving my pain a name and a treatment.

I can't distinguish between the beginning and the end, the ovum and the dregs. All the sadness that softens my musculature can be traced back to a chemical, hormonal disruption. In *Black, Black,*

Black, Luz invents a therapist to guide her through menopause. Dr. Bartoldi is an imaginary being who always speaks to her with deep respect, and as if dancing a slow waltz with her, he helps her move forward. I don't want to talk to any psychologists because no psychologist is *cleverer* than I am. Life is hard, and it gets harder as time passes. But I love and I am loved. As I frenetically seek words, pile them high, I need someone in a white lab coat to find a name for this roving and shape-shifting ailment—and to invent a painkiller for it. But sorry, there's no budget for that. Because it's fucking *natural*, isn't it? The ordeals of the female of the species are fucking natural.

In the meantime, it's up to Luz and me to drag ourselves out of bed every day and carry on.

I dream that I'm holding an eagle on my lap, trying to protect her. She's sick and afraid of me. She feels threatened and her talons scratch my chest. But she's too weak, or maybe she gradually becomes accustomed or resigned, or realizes that I'm her only chance for survival. I bite my lip to keep from crying out. She's causing me so much pain, but I don't want anyone to notice the bulge underneath my blouse. The eagle moves less and less. Every now and then I peek in at her. She's losing her feathers and the strength in her wings; her rigid wingspan has softened. She starts to resemble a dead chicken that I would normally stuff with tomatoes and lemon to roast in the oven. Pinkish drops of blood form around my nipples and spread. People start to stare. The eagle is about to die. She's fading. Upon analysis, it's just another vulgar metaphor for the helplessness of children. I don't have children, nor am I an eagle. I don't think so anyway.

I stop smoking, which helps save money. It doesn't make me feel any purer or more liberated. But I do notice that my stash of prescription drugs seems to be growing at an alarming rate.

Work commitments keep me traveling, and despite the tick gripping my heart I decide to keep going. I decide I'm not going to coddle myself or withdraw from daily life. But the truth is I'm not sure I can decide anything about anything. It's a kind of inertia, feeling trapped between the fantasy that we actually get to choose *anything* in life and the guilt for not listening to the messages our body sends us. As if we could just stop and exit the rat race whenever we felt like it. We can't. And even that is our fault. We get blamed for all of it.

Elvira Navarro, one of Spain's new generation of young women authors, describes something like this rat race guilt in her novel *La trabajadora* (*A Working Woman*). Women writers in Spain today understand the uncertainty of our lives during a global recession and brutal government austerity, and we write about it because it pains us; we write because we are women, because we have or we don't have a partner, because we have or we don't have a job, because we are white Spanish women, possibly feminist, possibly left wing. But our books aren't all written with the same words, and as a consequence, no, they aren't the same. *C'est dans l'air du temps.*

So I keep traveling. But when I'm alone in one of my hotel rooms, I start to imagine I'm about to have an episode. That my tick will jab me, and I won't be able to breathe. Today, this illusion is especially tragic, because the walls in this particular hotel room are painted a lovely sky-blue color. The room is infused with light and is very clean. Smells good. Small but well-appointed. Cozy. No pretense. But the episode leaves me cowering between the wall and the bed, while I try to concentrate on the lace curtains gently swaying in the breeze. How pretty is this hotel room in the south of Spain at siesta time, but the light filtering through the lace just makes me sad. I start to imagine how the tick will suck all the calcium out of my bones, as if my skeleton were a nutritious glass of milk or a freshwater spring. No one will come to help me.

But then my cell phone will start to ring, because my husband will be waiting for me at the station where I won't emerge from the train. My cell phone will ring, but I won't be able to hear it and he'll stand there helplessly. He'll look one way, then the other. He'll walk up and down the platform and in the waiting area. Meanwhile, I'll still be trapped between the wall and the bed, watching the curtains as the sun sets and my room goes dark.

But no. I rally. I go into the bathroom and put on lipstick. No one will ever know what an effort this is. Applying lipstick is my way of overcoming. Later, speaking at the book fair in this southern city, my performance is frankly magnificent. I talk about Luz and Dr. Bartoldi. No one in the audience can make out the tiny patch of red burning a hole in my chest. And tomorrow I'll be home. Again.

We go to my parents' house for lunch. My mother has prepared an old-fashioned, high-nutrition meal of lentils and sardines. Homemade and familiar. It's so hard to eat well when we go out to restaurants. Apparently, I've come to detest "heart-healthy" menus, dietary tyranny, and the cultural prestige awarded to successful chefs, and yet I do sometimes eat at restaurants with a few Michelin stars, and I do enjoy the eclectic and refined meals prepared for me by my friend Bienve, who makes beef stuffed with lobster meat or raviolis filled with the white shrimp from Huelva. Apparently, I also deplore the most obvious signs of a society in decline, such as celebrity chefs, recipes that use seaweed, and society's repugnance toward saturated fats. Nevertheless, I watch my weight, limit my portions, do general self-care—all the while licking the grease off my fingers. I feel the same about soap operas and certain other abominable TV shows, which I criticize but also watch. The burdens of my era are hard to bear. I acknowledge them, I try to resist them, and they defeat me. Pitiful.

Lentils and sardines. Classic. Now we just need fresh oranges for dessert. Thank goodness Mom feeds us—me, my husband, and my dad—like we're little cygnets, and she, the mother swan. Today she braided her hair across the crown of her head. She hates it when her white scalp shows through the strands of her hair after long hours leaning her head against the back of the armchair. After lunch my father cleans the dishes. He uses too much dish soap to scrub the pans. Too much blue product to polish the ceramic stovetop. Mom scolds him, tells him he doesn't do things right. But he ignores her and carries on, and she leaves the kitchen grumbling to go watch television. She gets so mad at him. *"Hombre, hombre, hombre,"* she repeats in a loop at the end of each indignant pronouncement, sometimes adding a "Fuck!" Mom gets mad a lot but gets over it quickly. The next day she gets mad again, likely for the same reasons, because at this stage of the game no one's going to change my father's stripes. Or maybe it's the opposite: only at this stage of the game can anyone change in a dramatic way, and my mother isn't wasting her energy. Mom also cries easily. Today she got very emotional when a picture in a magazine reminded her of her deceased dog.

When he's done cleaning up after lunch, my father goes off to his room and listens to jazz while making collages with photographs of smiley celebrities who annoy him. He cuts them out of the newspaper. He has a million Cristiano Ronaldos, Christine Lagardes, Eugenia Silvas, and others who smile, smile, smile. My father still knows his geometry, and on a little piece of paper he deploys it to draw concentric five-point stars that he colors in with orange, red, and yellow. His piece will be titled *Explosion in Valencia*. My mother comes up from behind and startles him. "Ramón, that's horrible."

"Not everything can be a masterpiece," he responds. There is hardly any space left, paintings and collages piled everywhere. Tiny little frames and large-format canvases: a giant chickpea, a sacramental coffeepot, an image of garbanzo stew cut into sections and pasted along the borders of the canvas, divided up, *contra naturam,* on a black background. The broth doesn't spill out. In another medium-sized piece, a raised fist clenches an artichoke. In the collages: children, sports figures, dignitaries, and the horror vacui of the political class. My father declares that it's his way of fighting Alzheimer's. My mother offers up another opinion: "Ramón, this one has come out really well." He looks at her skeptically: "Do you really think so?"

Later my mother laughs out loud watching a silly TV show, and after that the two of them play Scrabble, and no one can enter their little bubble. "You added up my points wrong." "I don't have any vowels." "That is not a word." "Yes, it is. Look it up." "Can I use *yets*, in the plural?" "No." "Why not? You just played *yesterdays*." My parents have become lexicographers in their old age.

Lately, my mother worries about my traveling. She feels sorry for me. I laugh it off, but after a while, her concern starts to become mine and I, too, feel sorry for myself. Safe at home, she's probably imagined horrors like airplanes in free fall, airport arrests, terrorism, infectious diseases, the off chance that I might consume some unhealthy saturated palm oil fats. Just thinking of me sitting alone at a boarding gate is enough. It kills her, though I laugh it off and remind her: "Mamá, I'm almost fifty years old." She stops to think about that for a moment and then seems even sadder. Her eyes well up with tears.

I promise to write everything that needs to be written about my parents while they can still read it. After they die, not one more word. Maybe writing about them like this now is an effort at cryogenic freezing. A spell to turn my parents into eternal beings. A preparation. Or vaccination. Not an homage. Not a monument. But a way to mitigate anticipated grief. I want to dominate pain as if it were a wild animal. Foreshadow the yellowing teeth. I don't know if my tactic will work. Preparing for the future could backfire. Sadden us. Infect us. "Honey, don't you need to be getting home?" my father teases me. Sometimes I think it's funny; other times it pisses me off. My husband and I finally head out, and as we go down in the elevator, I'm unsettled by all this sweetness and peace. I can't enjoy it. Because it always ends.

My parents' growing fragility penetrates my bones. It becomes my own fragility. I detest nature and the inexorable. I don't know how to live. And yet . . .

Sarinagara is a novel about grief by the French writer Philippe Forest. Forest's young daughter has died, and he seeks comfort in biographies, almost always tragic, by Japanese writers. He seeks comfort in reading and writing. In analogies and the gap between them. In the fusion of civilizations and the impossibility of melding into nothingness. Everything, even grief for the daughter who dies, eventually heals or rots away. *Sarinagara* means something akin to "and yet" in Japanese. Forest writes it to help him cling to life when it seems like there is nothing left to live for. *Everything is shit, my daughter has died, Paris is overcast, and I can hear the rats as they jump from one electric cable to another, and yet* . . . he discerns a point of light amid the darkness of the storm. It's the Mojácar Lighthouse, our medieval symbol of resistance and reconciliation. We are safe until the next tempest.

I understand Forest. It must be horrible to lose your little girl, and any argument that favors continued existence after that demonstrates the courage of whoever came up with it. I need *sarinagara* before anything really bad actually happens to me. In anticipation. Like someone who's built up a resistance to painkillers, which no longer work, and starts to seek prescriptions for a more poisonous pesticide. I write my own *sarinagara* without the funeral pomp. Later on, we will see.

MY CLAVICLE

The pain mutates as the days go by. The tick becomes a mouse that morphs in size and shape inside the bony cage of my ribs, and my mouse becomes a finch egg, then a disheveled little finch itself, a green finch, a finch whose bright colors fade even though it never quite dies. Fucking finch. The pain travels through my body, becoming a swimming fish. It swims, or more concretely, it creeps, crawls, scrapes, squeezes. It's chronic and stinks like the dirty water in a terrarium. The mossy stench coats my nasal passages, descends into my mouth, and penetrates into my stomach, lining it like a layer of dust on a dirty washrag. It turns my stomach. It never goes away.

My mother decides it might be helpful to remind me about all our deceased family members and how they died. My aunt Mari Loli died of cardiac arrest. My aunt Marisol died alone in her house, also of a heart attack, and nearly rotted in the heat, devoured by carpet mites. Uncle Bienve was just thirty-something when he died, leaving behind a wife and three children. Mari Loli, Marisol, Bienve . . . this is the branch of the family I most resemble—increasingly so as I age (a little old lady?)—and I confirm that I am drying up, just like Aunt Marisol. On my left arm I can now see two veins that were previously covered with flesh. It's revolting at first, then little by little I start to find them charming.

Mari Loli, Marisol, Bienve . . . Next, my mother lists the great-aunts and -uncles on my paternal grandmother's side who were diagnosed with heart disease. After hearing the description of my pain, she's determined to convince me to make an appointment with the cardiologist, pressing on with her catalog of dead relatives, flipping through it like a photo album: her grandmother Claudia's throat cancer, my grandmother Rufina's brain tumor. My mother, who's anxious and doesn't sleep well, insists on reminding me of our gloomy family medical history. She means well.

I have a wild dream about my mother. She's wearing a print bikini and lying on a bale of hay. In the sun. With a Cordobés-style straw hat on her head. In her right hand she holds a glass of cognac; in her left hand, she pinches a cigarette between her thumb and her index finger. She doesn't balance it, like a lady, between her index and middle fingers. She clutches it like a metalworker, her eyes heavily made up, and in my dream, she looks like she's just thirty years old, though slightly less beautiful than she is in real life. The fact is this: my mother is one of the few people who can make me laugh, even in a dream.

I just learned today that in the 1950s my uncle Segundo, the one from Roturas, committed suicide by hanging himself from a rafter in the attic of his house. He'd just been diagnosed with an incurable disease. His wife, my aunt Nazaria, used to treat my father's sore throat by wrapping dirty socks around his neck. Remedies and pharmacopeias were different back then. My father describes Uncle Segundo to me with a literary reference underscoring his love of life: "He was a perfect Sancho Panza." My mother's take is harsher: "He was a drunk."

Not too long ago, learning this new tidbit of family dirt would have inspired me to start writing. Typically some long and complicated story. But today the news is just another data point. One piece of a medical history puzzle that makes me think of Ernest Hemingway and his granddaughter Margaux, who both died by suicide. I was reassured when my father told me that Segundo was the adopted brother of my great-grandmother Catalina, a hospice worker from Bilbao. Ergo, there's no shared hemophilia, or consanguinity, or blue blood, and I really should censor my obtuse propensity to be bookish one minute and crude the next, although that does essentially define my style. At first, writing is natural, like the smell of moss in a rural winery. Later it starts to reek of commercialism, like slick packaging in a high-end supermarket.

When I write—when we write—we can't forget our material condition. That's why I think every text is autobiographical and that sometimes our disguises—the sinuous, translucent fabrics that cover our bodies—are less modest than naked declarations. I'm not interested in photoshopped selfies. I care more about the unedited facial expression, before language cleans it up, whitening each tooth and smoothing each wrinkle. I'm more interested in the pipe than *une pipe* that's not a pipe. An autobiography is the consecration of reality and of spring, not the number of stitches required to suture it into a story. My style reflects my fractured, menopausal insides. And this discomfort in certain regions of my body—flatulence, hemorrhoids, fibroids—may be clouding my intelligence. Or maybe not. What I can say is that I still care a lot about how much I'm going to be paid for my work. This very book, for example, which I am now editing and which is starting to scare the shit out of me.

A journalist asks, "What inspires you to write?"

Why do so many people ask me this? Because it's a genuinely interesting question, or because nobody has any imagination anymore when it comes to asking questions? Or answering them? Whatever anyone asks, my answer is always the same: I explain why I write and what I write about. I mechanically replay the answer that today resonates more strongly than ever: "I write about what pains me." I repeat this in five, ten, two hundred interviews. "I write about what pains me." Today I clearly see that writing seeks to name and impose order on chaos. On the chaos of nature, the chaos of demented cells that resist death, the chaos that lurks inside the order of social structures. Writing scrapes away at entropy like a spoon scrapes away at the prison wall. It amputates gangrenous limbs. It identifies the evil of diseases so they can be healed. Writing makes everything just a little bit clearer by tidily tying the giant squid's swirling tentacles with a red velvet ribbon, collecting the black ink it expels into the depths of the abyss, and organizing it into letters of the alphabet.

Over time—almost four months now—the diagnostic hypotheses produced by my visits to various doctors have shifted: lung cancer, overexertion, anxiety, heart disease, mitral valve stenosis, esophageal diverticulum, toothache, fungus, nothing. The tests and their results come back slowly because it's "not urgent." But I'm incapable of thinking of anything else. I search everywhere endlessly, trying to find the words to name things.

No one mentions the word *menopause*. It's a talisman, a taboo.

No one mentions the word *menopause* or bothers to explain exactly why—just before my body experiences its minuscule combustion, that hiss of the match as it catches fire, that surge in temperature, which in my case is far from a furnace—why in that instant just before do I feel something is about to go terribly wrong, that something bad is about to happen. I experience a nanosecond of profound, cosmic discomfort, much more tremendous and depressing than simply losing my ability to accurately distinguish hot from cold. This tiny apocalypse of hormones also makes it difficult to sleep or have regular bowel movements, which the homeopaths, naturopaths, and creative marketers take advantage of in turn. This cosmic sorrow heralds the vulgarity of the hot flash. A warning that puts me on guard, like the aura that's reportedly experienced just before an epileptic seizure. Or by a werewolf just noticing there's a full moon.

MY CLAVICLE

One day I can't take it anymore and I break into a fit of sobs in front of the doctor at the urgent care clinic. "What are you afraid of?" she asks. I say, "Of being sick. Of not being able to work." The second part of my answer feeds into my fear that maybe I am completely crazy. I look at my husband, who always accompanies me to the doctor. He swallows hard. The doctor gives me a hug. I don't like being hugged by strangers, even when I need consolation. Now that I think of it, I don't like to be hugged by people I know, either. Between my hiccups and her interrogations, I confirm my shocking admission by repeating it to her: "I'm afraid I won't be able to work." I've stopped crying now. I don't want kind words or a prescription for sedatives. I'm sick from my fear of getting sick and sick from worrying about it. Sick with fear that the world is collapsing and that my illness will keep me from paying the bills. For a moment I'm convinced my fear is rational and I'm condemned to forever think in riddles.

The doctor bypasses protocol and sends me to get an emergency chest X-ray. I press myself against the surface of the X-ray machine. I try to boost my courage with the admission: "I'm a little scared." The nurse says, "Of course you are." The nurse's choice of words, meant perhaps to calm me, tortures me instead.

In less than an hour, we have eliminated the possibility of lung cancer.

Things are complicated. And simple. All at the same time.

I care a lot about what my father thinks, and no, that's not Freudian or codependent. It's called respect. Love.

They say it's best to have children when you're still young. It's not true in our case. My father can't bear seeing his daughter so vulnerable. He can't tolerate my anguish. So instead he calls me crazy. He says it with affection—it just slips out—but when he glimpses my reaction, the look on my face, he clearly wishes he could cut out his tongue. Maybe he's just protecting himself against his own pain at seeing me like this, every day more shrunken, a thin thread of a voice, mournful eyes. So my father lashes out at me—and I don't know if he does it to distance himself or because he doesn't understand any of this; he's also a wounded man who accepts that an injury is real only if it results from actual hand-to-hand combat, and he refuses to acknowledge pain from anything that isn't transformative: the tadpoles that become frogs or a kidney that starts to fail. "But what about science?" I wonder, in order to steel myself. But we're too late for science. And I know it.

Now he avoids my gaze in case tears well up in his eyes. He doesn't want to look at me in case he feels the uncomfortable urge to slap me, which of course he's never done. *Wake up! Snap out of it! Live!* he's saying to me without really saying it. *Stop working out, stop obsessing with your body, stop being such a drama queen, such a worm. Go live your life!* It drives my father crazy when I do my ab exercises around him. "Unbelievable." My pain leaves me feeling horribly guilty. My pain is a failure, one that I mustn't allow. Irrefutable proof of my weak intelligence.

Maybe all this is punishment for failing to perpetuate the family line. If I had children, today I'd be worrying about a hypothetical motorcycle accident, an unwanted pregnancy, incipient symptoms of leukemia manifested by a little bit of pain in the molars and low-grade fevers. I'd be worried about the facts of life and the lack of decent job opportunities. I'd be less selfish, and my (I think we can all agree) impressive knowledge of anatomy—my scapula, my trigeminal nerve, my conoid tubercle; they all hurt—would shift from obsessively observing my own body to permanently evaluating my little ones'. Above all, I'd be worried about how my children will make their way. How in God's name they'd be able to earn a living. And I would fly from the nest even more compulsively than I do now, if that's even possible, to bring home straw, breadcrumbs, and tiny insects.

MY CLAVICLE

My loved ones say, with affection, "You've got to get past this. You're a smart woman." When I realize that I can't get past it, that I'm still struggling to breathe and there's still a tick stuck in my chest, I notice that all my intelligence disappears. I babble. Also, my desire to work is fading. I'm letting my loved ones down.

And yet, when I map out my packed schedule, it's clear that I'm completely successful. I have an amazing life. Next week I'll be in Paris. Then I'll be on Cap de Formentor, Mallorca, and I'll stroll through gardens where Charlie Chaplin, Grace Kelly, and Agatha Christie once walked. I'll cross the pond to México and drink mezcal with Paola while we sample small dishes that have been listed as UNESCO Intangible Cultural Heritage (though I don't quite understand the word *intangible* as it's applied to guacamole). I'll meet with a ton of media, I'll say whatever I want, I'll appear on TV. There is and there will be documentary evidence of all these adventures. My dreams have come true. I hope I don't suffocate. I hope I can sleep. No, I can't get sick.

MY CLAVICLE

Ever had to search for words to describe pain, which is a symptom, to help doctors diagnose the problem? The doctor begs you: "You have to help me." The expression on your face is a plea as you dig through the collection of words stored in your memory. "My pain is..." *A knot, a tie, a bow tie, a cramp, an absence, an inverted hollow, a spoonful of air, a void in a vacuum, a metaphysical target, suction, oppression, a rodent bite, a duck bite, a weasel bite, a zap, vertigo, a sting, a scratch, a prickly bramble, a dust ball, grit in my teeth, a stone in my throat* or *my lungs, the taste of blood and metal, a torn ligament, an electric shock, shortness of breath, dry mouth.* So many words, but I can't speak any of them. I know this language and its rhetoric well. But I'm tongue-tied. I can't explain myself, and my heart is pounding. It's hitting 160 beats per minute. Tachycardia. I look into the doctor's eyes with mute desperation. There are no metaphors that can possibly express my pain.

Juan insists on seeing me—and on lending me money if I need it. I don't know where he's gotten the idea I need money, but my friend's generosity moves me as much as it bothers me. He's worried about me, and that makes me worried, too, as he offers two referrals to help me with my Hydra-headed health concerns. As it turns out, the decision is like choosing between a honeydew melon and a cantaloupe, almost the same but different: Juan's brother, a traumatologist, and Mariano, a psychiatrist, who for a time treated Juan's eating disorder. A doctor for my body and a doctor for my soul. But Juan warns me that his brother the body doctor is very brusque—like all traumatologists apparently—and Mariano the soul doctor is always clear, direct, and contextual. Mariano's professional profile is impressive, but his name dissuades me. It may come as no surprise that I'm onomastically sensitive—that is, I place a lot of stock in the etymology of proper names—and I could never feel confident seeing a psychiatrist related, at least in name, to the hypermasculine Mars, Roman god of war.

After three months of no in-person contact, my husband and I meet up with Juan at a terrace bar. We drink beer and white wine; we talk about how hard it is to evaluate whether you might have a psychological problem when society is so intolerant of psychotherapy. The health care industry is also intolerant of the idea that the root cause of a physical malady might sometimes be psychological.

They're irritated by those Freudian psychiatrists who obsess about the impact of family on mental and physical health. "Mariano isn't like that!" Juan is adamant. Mariano is a materialist. So am I, and so are my parents and my husband, the people I care for most and who care for me. My mother was the only religious one for a while until she married an atheist. Not that religion ever did her any good, as she's always been a pessimist. My mother and I are both genetically unhappy. DNA downers.

Some things are hard for me to put up with. Foolish melancholy, for one. People who get all emotional. In our family, we think depression must be related to thyroid dysfunction. Or idleness. Too much time to sit around twiddling your fingers.

That's what's so devastating for me these days, this loss of confidence in my own strength. I've always been strong, and I've always been confident, and I keep thinking that I should be able to overcome this, and if I fail, it's my own fault. Everything can be overcome with time, planning, and hard work. Rationality, please, rationality. I'm skeptical about the loss of control as we age, and I feel sorry for myself when I can't remember names or when my diminishing aerobic stamina keeps me from taking the stairs two by two. "That's a problem." Juan takes a sip of his white wine.

My husband chain-smokes through the entire conversation, recognizing each and every sentiment of each and every word, but clearly not sure he wants to hear them spun together into a speech. I know he's skeptical of these verbal exercises that expose your inner world, that put private images on display. It's possible my husband is afraid that talking about my condition will make it worse, but I carry on anyway, explaining how much I suffer when it feels like I'm exhausting my capacity for work, work being essential to my practice of self-exploitation, in which lies the germ of my happiness. I can't bear to show weakness in public, because the public is always the enemy. I'm ashamed to ask for help, and maybe it wasn't a great idea to meet up with Juan and put my weakness on display. Although at least today I've pulled myself together. Clean hair, a touch of lipstick, sunglasses.

Paying someone to get me out of this hole, this tiny and frivolous hole, just seems immoral to me. Ultimately, I say no thanks to Juan's suggestion. Does that make me arrogant? Or is it just an aversion to self-help literature, the power of positive thinking, and the kind of gurus of whom, though I deny it, I am also a victim. At some point, inside my head, a dichotomy emerges: I'm fragile, and at the same time my strength is titanic. I've said it before: there's no one in the world smarter than me, at least when it comes to things related to me. I don't believe in asking for help, being needy. I don't believe in osteopathy or in psychotherapists. I am, after all, a Spanish woman.

Juan howls with laughter.

Those of us who experience an imaginary illness can become so self-absorbed that we end up destroying others through neglect. Disregard. We forget about the rest of the world and its emergencies. We forget about the suffering of children with cancer: their little bald heads, dark circles under their eyes, their veins. We also forget about the child laborers who pick jasmine petals to put in a basket that never ever fills. We forget the children who live right nearby who go to school without breakfast or even lunch. We selfishly forget them. Or maybe rather than forgotten, their suffering has already infected us, pierced our skin like a splinter, entering our bloodstream. Maybe those of us with imaginary illnesses have become victims alongside the truly ill, who would gouge out our eyes with a teaspoon if they could. We're exhausted. What horrible human beings we are, we women of the imaginary unwell.

Crunching the numbers. We've paid off the mortgage. No children. Just the two of us. We pay seventy euros a month for our cell phones and internet connection because we got an amazing deal. Our condo association fee is forty-eight euros a month plus thirty euros for water. The electricity bill is around thirty euros a month. Natural gas costs us about one hundred euros a month in winter. I pay a self-employment tax of almost four hundred euros, and now that his unemployment has been used up, my husband pays a self-employment tax of almost three hundred. We eat fish and vegetables. We don't eat processed meat, or sausages, or commercial baked goods, because we both have high cholesterol. Grocery shopping isn't cheap. Maybe four hundred euros a month. My husband smokes and cigarettes are expensive. I pay membership dues in professional organizations and political parties, for foundations that support the Historical Memory Recovery Project. I buy little tissue packets from the poor. And, inexcusably, I throw coins into the hats of street musicians. It's true that I don't buy books. Everyone gives them to me. But we like to go to the movies and occasionally eat out in a good restaurant. Our friends' lifestyles are more extravagant than ours. Most of our friends are professionals and specialists who hold important positions in the public or private sector. Sometimes we loan money, with no expectation it will ever be repaid, to family members who are worse off than we are. Recently,

I've been seeing a physical therapist who charges me 180 euros for five sessions. These are some of our expenses. We have a bit of savings.

Our income derives from a variety of sources: occasional collaborations with news publications that range from fifty to three hundred euros gross each; teaching classes in public and private schools; speaking appearances that sometimes pay a thousand euros and sometimes pay absolutely nothing; book advances that are never that substantial; author royalties that sometimes exist and sometimes don't; serving as a judge for literary awards. The jobs multiply and, as with design, form follows function; this enumeration of my jobs is not an affectation but a necessity. Our financial precariousness is reflected in this fractured accumulation of so many different jobs, which have to be combined to reach and maintain a single goal: solvency. Everything is always up in the air. Some job offers are symptomatic of this: one journal asked me to write fifty-eight pieces a year, for which it would pay me a total of 1,200 euros gross. We, the offspring of waiters, mechanics, farmworkers, even first-generation liberal professionals, are the proletariat of letters. Long gone are the days when culture was an element of upward mobility. It's like we're literary Stakhanovites, trapped in a Soviet worker culture that reveres hard labor as its own reward. I'm reminded of Charlie Chaplin in his 1936 movie, *Modern Times*, comically struggling to keep up with the speeding conveyer belt on the machine workers' assembly line. Contemporary life consists of working all day and then feeling guilty when you aren't working. It's disproportionate, the yawning gap between effort and remuneration that obliges me to multiply the number of jobs I take on to maintain my modest lifestyle. I have to say yes to everything for fear that they won't ask again if I say no, and because I do the math and I can see that the coordinates on our budgetary axis are headed inexorably toward zero.

My inside has always been my outside, and my soul, my flesh. I profess this faith and it's my religion.

My pain is a script written when I'm afraid I won't be able to pay the bills or support myself in my old age without smelling like an old woman. I think this confession is completely impudent, and absolutely necessary.

MY CLAVICLE

I am commissioned to write a story. I write it. It's published by Demipage in a collection of stories about prescription drugs. I live in a vicious circle. I'm being completely honest.

"We Seek a Poppy That Won't Wilt"
Marta Sanz

1. In the Águilas station I take a picture of my feet while I wait for the bus that will take me to Almería. There, I'll wait two hours for another bus that leaves at four o'clock for Málaga. When I get to Málaga, I'll take a taxi to San Roque, where tomorrow I'll give a talk about love. The taxi driver will point out the five-star hotels that line the highway connecting Ojén, Marbella, and Estepona. He'll reveal a secret to me: "I used to be the chauffer for Mario Conde's first wife. Such an elegant woman. Gorgeous." I'll remember that the otherwise lucky lady (wife of the disgraced banker turned writer) died prematurely from breast cancer. I'll spend the night in a five-star hotel with a gorgeous garden. Beyond the garden is one of the most polluted bays in Spain. Petronor's smokestacks. Or Campsa's. Below the surface: radioactive submarines. In the distance, the Rock of Gibraltar and its crazed monkeys.

At night, in bed, I'll notice a strange vibration in my gut, and my eyes will open wide as saucers. I'll have toast with olive oil for breakfast. As soon as I finish my talk in San Roque, another taxi driver will take me back to Málaga. I don't know if I'll prefer the first driver or this one. I don't know if I'll prefer the simulated familiarity forged during the drive out or the effort required to chat with a stranger along the same path as the day before. Or to talk about politics. "There are too many bureaucrats." "The Reds murdered priests." "People who don't have jobs just don't want to work." In Málaga, I'll eat, I'll wait, I'll drink a beer, and I'll catch the bus to Almería, where I'll have to wait another two hours to get the bus that will take me back to Águilas. Starting at six in the afternoon, the Almería bus station will start to fill up with people I don't want to see. People who will make me feel too white, too clean, too rich. That last bit about feeling too rich seems crazy. And an expression of guilt. I'll arrive at ten thirty at night to the very spot where I am now waiting to start my journey. My husband and my parents will come to pick me up, and my father will get confused and then frightened because he'll think I'm on the bus from Cartagena instead of the one from Almería. Once past his fright, we'll all go to the amusement park, and I'll ride the Happy Kangaroo.

2. Before setting off on my journey from the Águilas bus depot, I take a picture of my feet (see photo). I'm wearing my pink ballet flats. They seem innocent enough, but they chafe.

There's an oil stain on the floor. A fly, stupefied by the heat, perches on my jeans. Sleepy. Myself, I take lorazepam to sleep at night.

3. I'm in the Águilas bus depot anticipating how tired I'm going to be when I get back tomorrow. At the moment, I'm not aware that the next day I'll go to the amusement park or that I'll have garlic potatoes for dinner. The trip is exhausting, besides which I can never sleep well the first night I stay in a hotel. Especially in one subjected to all kinds of toxic emissions. I've developed something of a tolerance to muscle relaxants and sleeping pills. But I never, under any circumstances, take more than one a day. Nor do I let a day go by without taking one.

4. In the Águilas bus depot, a man's cell phone rings. It plays the Spanish national anthem. No official lyrics, but over the years for several generations of Spaniards, some unofficial

verses penned by the Franco supporter José María Pemán have lodged in our ears: "Viva España! Lift your arms high, you sons of Spain who have risen again." A woman walks behind one of the buses just as it starts to back out. She's about to be run over. Someone swallows a scream along with their saliva. The woman, who's about to die, crushed beneath the wheels of the bus, doesn't flinch. She continues walking through the bus lane. As if it were nothing. I can't tell if she's oblivious or stubborn. Beside me, another woman turns to her husband and says, "I have to go to the gynecologist." I glance at her. I sniff her out. I weigh her up. Take her measure and try to guess her age. All out of the corner of my eye. She must have an actual problem, because she seems past the age for regular gynecological checkups. The couple falls silent. Then she says, "Those Black women have amazing bodies." The heat becomes stifling. The flies are eating us alive.

5. Heath Ledger's father has just declared that his son is to blame for his own death. He used a mixture of oxycodone, hydrocodone, diazepam, and doxylamine. Holy Mother of God. I suppose there comes a moment when nothing seems to work anymore, and we have to don our lab coats and start combining potions. We seek a poppy that won't wilt. We seek to pass, for a little while, unnoticed. Heath Ledger and me. But mostly Heath Ledger. But when I sleep well, I wake up with a song on my lips. Songs by my favorite Latin artists: Las Grecas, Shakira and Alejandro Sanz, Tahúres Zurdos. I

make up the lyrics as I go, but I sing with gusto. I want to be enormously, hyperesthetically happy. At night, when I can't sleep, I think of death and all the turbulence in the world. The electricity goes out and the flashlights on everybody's phone fails. My bones ache when I get out of bed. My mouth is dry. I don't feel like talking. It weighs on me, all these files, all this work.

6. In the Águilas bus depot, I urgently need to pee. I stop taking pictures of my feet and make my way to a small room where a woman is mopping the floor with water and bleach. "Where do you think you're going, ma'am?" The cleaning woman, underpaid and undervalued, reigns supreme over her one area of dominion. She glares suspiciously at me. I disgust her. "The restroom, please?" My voice, as thin as threads of candied egg yolk, is a holdover from my childhood, still embedded in my vocal cords. When I was a little girl, I slept with the light on. I checked the closets. I woke up at any little noise. They'd give me hot milk with sugar. "In the back." The bathroom is clean, but there's no toilet paper. There's no lock on the door. My piss steams as it hits the bleach sterilizing the bottom of the toilet. I stand up before the toxic vapors touch me. I don't want any chemical burns on my mucous tissues and my intestinal flora. The reek of cleanliness penetrates everything in here. Pretty horrible for anyone with sensitive skin. The woman ignores me as I walk out. She's talking on her phone and her tone is unpleasant there, too. How do I

cope with this disregard? These insults? I sometimes wonder. Although, really, it could be a lot worse. The loudspeaker at the Águilas bus depot (see photo) announces that the bus to Almería, arriving from Cartagena, is delayed. My stomach churns as I imagine missing my connection to Málaga. I need the money from this talk and it's making me nervous, but no one notices. I project outward calm and tranquility.

7. Yes, I am completely aware that lorazepam in large doses can be deadly. I'm familiar with the case of twelve-year-old Asunta Basterra, found strangled by the side of the road with a massive dose of Orfidal, the high-end, nongeneric version of lorazepam, in her system. The girl's adoptive parents were convicted of anesthetizing her with the drug then murdering her. True crime stories are like a drug, in a way. I hear *Orfidal*, and I think black-and-white orchids, Orchidales, orchitis, swollen testicles, pure protein, egg yolk, an orfeón of xylophone players; I hear *Orfidal* and see

Orpheus trying to rescue Eurydice from hell, springtime forever held hostage, and, finally, Morpheus taking us onto his lap and cradling us like infant patients, drool dribbling from the corners of our mouths. Lack of sleep is deadly, but so is eating the witch's poisoned apple. I am aware that I take a drug that has the power to kill. That said, I don't dislike the idea that I can master the threat.

8. I remember how one night my father-in-law took a sedative to help him sleep and ended up sleepwalking. He didn't even recognize his wife, who led him by the arm back to bed. Some older people are very sensitive to medication, but others seem immune to overdose no matter how many pills they pop. Other than that, my father-in-law was healthy. In the end, I think it was his fear of death that made him want to die. He was always thinking about his age, counting the years on his fingers. Once he started to believe death was near, he died. Just like that. I always understood him, because I know all too well the morose thoughts insomnia can bring on. The inability to cope with overwork or too much time on your hands. Lorazepam is a family drug for us. Hereditary. My father-in-law took it, my grandfather, my mother. I take it, and even though I'm an only child, I can see that I'm part of a growing family of self-medicators. I wonder if this is a genetic or environmental problem. Nature versus nurture. Material or historical? Two grand words sadly used in conjunction.

9. On the bus to Almería, a woman boards and pays the fare with ten-cent coins. Dressed head to toe in black, it's immediately clear she doesn't speak Spanish, and she smiles at the driver uncomprehendingly. "If you pay like this, my Moorish queen, we'll all be here until tomorrow." In my imagination I see her walking through the tables at a terrace restaurant, collecting those coins from kind strangers who drop them in her little plastic cup. She looks at the driver wanting to be obliging, pretending to understand, yes, yes, yes. The bus starts up, and the countryside is gorgeous, studded with ravines and cliffs, just like Juan Goytisolo describes in *Campos de Níjar*. But I focus on things that remain within the confines of our vehicle's shatterproof windows: a few seats ahead of me, three or four girls are looking at the photos on their phones, drinking Coke, and eating candy (see furtive photo). I'm a woman of serene appearance, and I bless the scientists who created anesthesia, lorazepam, and sleeping pills.

10. A few months ago: As I enter the outpatient clinic to get some test results, I'm so nervous that my heart starts racing 150 beats per minute. I haven't been able to sleep, thinking about what the results might show. The doctor notices I'm nervous and recommends I take three lorazepam per day. She says if I start to feel really terrible, I should put one under my tongue. "It's bitter, but it's a godsend." She asks if I'm working and traveling a lot, and I tell her yes. She reviews my brief and recent medical history: "I see you've stopped smoking." For the first time, I get to feel pleased with myself at the doctor's office. I've done something that's good and healthy. Something that requires sacrifice. Ergo, I am morally good. I don't castigate my poor little body, even though I castigate myself. Indeed, I stopped smoking. But for some reason this leads to interrogation: "And why?" she asks. Not the question I expected. I have to think about it. I tell the truth: "I was afraid." The doctor contemplates me with a look of amusement. "Aha." She continues: "I smoke. Do you know why?" I shake my head no. "I'm not afraid." I congratulate her. Seeing a woman doctor helps a lot of women feel less afraid. More and more women all the time. Men, too. More and more people also chew their fingernails and eat yogurt for dinner. And yet still they suffocate because they work too much or can't get a job. I never take the three lorazepam that the doctor prescribes. Only one at night so I can sleep. At first it works, I sleep, but I also have bizarre nightmares. Black-and-white orchids. Mosquitoes hovering

over water in a barrel. At first, I sleep, but then I build up my tolerance, and the dose loses its effect. I keep taking it because I think it will be worse if I stop. Sometimes I think lorazepam blurs the days together, like blots of oil slowly merging across a paper towel or spilled ink creeping across the page. But then there are other times when it feels like spreading a soothing balm on a burn.

11. At the bar in the Almería bus stop, I order a beer. A man next to me asks if my name is Ana. "Yes, sure. Ana." He shows me his phone. He wants to erase a message, but he doesn't know how. I don't dare touch his phone myself. I say, "Go up, now down, yes, like that, on top, no, not there, touch the middle." Suddenly, I hear myself and think, *Shut up*. The man is very drunk, but finally, between the two of us, we manage to delete the message. It was sent by the cell phone company. "Are you an archaeologist?" Absolutely, I say. Always have been. He smiles, glances at my bag, and heads to the toilet. I grab my bag and slip stealthily toward the door. I disappear from his life. I'm a woman, traveling alone, in a bus depot. I'm almost fifty. I have eyes in the back of my head. And my ass. I seem to attract the oddballs and the delinquents. The irredeemable alcoholics. Slinking away like a cautious cartoon cat, I slide out of the station with my back to the wall. It never changes. With apologies to God, Almería, Andalucía, and Spain, it's still very tricky traveling alone here as a woman. "Yes, yes. Of course I'm an archaeologist." It is still tricky to

be a woman in this world—first world, second world, third world, whatever you want to call it—in my world. In my sleepless lorazepam purgatory. My disrupted, glazed over universe. Lorazepam is a sad drug.

12. When I don't want to be found, I bury myself in my books. Joan Medford, the protagonist in *The Cocktail Waitress*, a posthumously published novel by James M. Cain, takes thalidomide as a sedative. Perhaps she's also used thalidomide to murder a few of her lovers. God, of course, imposes retribution. At the end of the novel, rich and exonerated of murder charges, Joan Medford gets pregnant. She imagines the birth of a perfect baby girl but suffers terrible morning sickness and decides to take some of her leftover thalidomide to offset it. In the last lines of the story Joan prays her little girl will be spared the cruelties she herself suffered in life, never imagining her daughter will likely be born without legs and will need to be pushed across the polished tiles of their mansion in a wheelchair her whole life. I, on the other hand, still possess my legs, and in the Almería bus depot I photograph them from an amorphous and disconcerting angle (see eerie photo). Here's the thing: the same drug can sedate or kill, alleviate or amputate.

13. I continue on my journey, and tomorrow, on my way back on the night bus that travels along the section of highway between Los Lobos and San Juan de los Terreros, at least three bats strike the windshield of the bus. I'm the only passenger on board, with a very young driver who pulls up to each bus stop even though there's no one waiting to board and then guns the engine to get underway again (for which I'm grateful, eager as I am to get home). The bats hit the windscreen, and the young driver says, "Every night it's the same." He explains: "They're bats." He pauses, then speaks again: "Because it's nighttime, so they can't be birds,

right?" I purse my lips and swallow my response. The driver is just a boy who wants me to say that the stiff dogs lying in the ditches are just sleeping. I'd like to be able to console him: *There, there. It's okay. Shush now, there are no diseases, no death, no catastrophes, no swindlers or monsters. There are no angry, mop-wielding women cleaning bathrooms for three hundred euros a month. Just me, heading home from earning a day's wages. Shush now, little one, take a pill. It's okay, it's okay.* But it's not, really. It's not okay. Because I know, but I don't say, that some bird species are nocturnal. And I have so much work to do. And I can't sleep.

I tell my husband about all of this. He tries to act natural while reading my stories, and he says, "That's hilarious! An archaeologist!" We communicate well with each other, but I know that deep down he's not laughing at all, and it bothers him that some of the things I write about might be true. I'm not convinced that communicating with your partner is a healthy thing to do. Still, he calms me. Until later, when he can't help but ask how I'm feeling. "You okay? Is the pain any better today? Does it hurt more or less than a little while ago?" My husband's questions make it impossible to forget my symptoms. They make me listen to myself again, down to the tiniest little whistle of my lungs. Sometimes I'd like to blame him. But I can't. Because the pain really is there, even when I pretend not to feel it.

MY CLAVICLE

Whole new elements of my being are appearing that didn't exist before. The tick, which is like the head of a pin. The pain that feels like rasping. I walk my fingers along the area between my throat and my sternum, as if pressing the keys on a wind instrument. A bassoon. A clarinet. It hurts, and the pain is not diminished by the drugs for depression or insomnia. It's not anything about my life that's making me unhappy. It's this darkness inside my body.

I live in a paradox. On the one hand, I must seem like a terribly cruel woman to expose my loved ones to this public scrutiny. It's an act of wickedness, which my family tolerates without reproach, demonstrating the depth of their love. On the other hand, if I didn't write about my personal experiences, if I strategically manipulated what's familiar to seem foreign, I'd feel like a coward. And in the end, that manipulation might create a painful sense of doubt in those around me, who would wonder if they recognized themselves in my writing. While the doubt would be like a protective helmet for me, it would *still* mortify those I love.

For those of us who have the impulse to write, both paths—the biological and the cosmetic—are a mistake. I'm not bothered about the cosmetic path I haven't been taking these days, but I do worry about any pain my impertinent portrayal of family and friends might cause. *Sincerity, honesty,* and *authenticity* are words that litter the semantic field of evil acts. So, too, confessions, accusations, denunciations, and anonymous tips.

My writing is an uninterrupted assault. In a conspiracy of pleasingly blasphemous words and anatomical language, my writing strips us bare, both me and others, young and old. I tear off our clothes, exposing our blemishes in a search for our immense beauty. And I find it.

The pain is ruining my writing. It's colonizing my brain, leaving no room for anything else and making me vigilant but stupid at the same time. The pain is wrecking my writing, and I'm furious with myself as I suddenly realize that I'm writing as if I were an actual *hypochondriac*. I've adopted the jargon of hypochondria; it's what they expect of me. But today, I'm rebelling. I am not a hypochondriac. I am not depressed. I'm in pain. I have an actual condition and I own it. And, yes, I complain about it.

I'm an open book these days—as demonstrated by the latest freelance offer that's come in, which is clearly mocking my condition with the invitation to curate a book about literary cures. (A curator, mind you, is a person who takes care of something.) The book is called *The Novel Cure*, written in English, and its adaptation into other languages requires the attention of an author to write in the language of the translation a prolog and introduction appropriate to a work about healing.". The thesis is that literature cures the common cold, brain fog, and schizophrenia. It's an amiable undertaking about the possible benefits of reading literature. Novels are a warm poultice, a mustard plaster on your chest, a cup of herbal tea, my grandmother Rufi's chicken soup. Myself, I prefer books that give you styes. That carve stigmata on your palms. That catch in your throat and take your breath away.

The gods are taunting me.

But, as always, I don't have the luxury of saying no.

MY CLAVICLE

I'm in such bad shape that even my mother can't seem to help me, despite her best efforts. She's trying to stay positive, which is hard for her to do. As I've said, she and I share downer DNA, a genetic predisposition to pessimism, despite having everything we could possibly need to be happy. I know her well. We are malcontents, but my mother, with almost superhuman effort, spurred on by love for me, searches for the cause of my suffering: menopause, emphysema, my grandmother's heart disease, or the strange heart conditions that did away with my great-grandparents at an early age, thirty, forty years old. My mother considers whether it might be flatulence, rheumatism, celiac disease, or hyperthyroidism. "Are your eyes bulging out? That's a symptom," she says. My mother seems to know everything that could provoke shortness of breath and chest pain. But she doesn't want to think about other possible underlying causes for my issues. About problems that can't be fixed.

Pain isn't as intimate as it's made out to be. It's a visible spasm in your being that affects how your loved ones see you. Everyone agrees you look unwell, and your certainty that everyone notices the dark circles under your eyes, the sallow hue of your skin, the bitter turn of your mouth, the increasingly pronounced shrinkage and curving of your spine, accentuates all of it. Such helpful feedback comes in from friends: "The same thing happened to me." "I had to be hospitalized." "I'm sure it's nothing." "Agoraphobia." "You have to rule out the physical causes." "Don't even think about antianxiety meds." "You should take sleeping pills. You can't go without sleep." "Hypochondria is a symptom of depression." "You work too hard." "Don't you think you might be exaggerating just a bit?" "It's menopause." "Don't let them do that test on you where they freeze your heart." "I know a good psychiatrist." "Your eyes are so baggy." "This will pass." "I'm worried about you." "I'm with you."

MY CLAVICLE

On the street I bump into Javier, and when he asks me how I'm doing I notice that I have suddenly become much smaller and weaker. In his presence, my skin cracks like paper scorched by the sunlight. This morning, I dyed my hair black, and you can see traces of the dye staining my scalp, forehead, and temples. It makes me think of the protagonist in *Death in Venice* who slowly decomposes on the beach. I want desperately to disappear.

My husband asks, "Does it hurt?" And even though on this day, at this precise instant, the pain is slightly more bearable, I say, "It hurts a lot." I like to watch how his features fall and sadness engulfs him. How he aches with my pain. It's not good to get used to excessive happiness, to get your hopes up. Later I feel bad about this, and that comforts me. In any case, I'm skirting around the central question here, because, in the end, I can't forget that the pain persists. And even if it doesn't, it might return at any moment.

MY CLAVICLE

My GP sends me to the gynecologist, pulmonologist, cardiologist, and rheumatologist. They perform many tests on me that later I will use to write books. This one, for example. They do blood analysis, cytology tests, mammograms, chest X-rays, a spirometry test, an electrocardiogram, more blood analysis, and a bone density test. I go to my appointments, and I smile, thinking about how much we crazy ladies are costing Social Security.

Occasionally, I wonder what came first, the chicken or the egg. My Cartesian skepticism questions whether the sadness came first and then somatized to my rib cage, or whether the stinging pain in my ribs created the sadness that now borders on the pathological. As I think about my issues, I consider the meaning of the words *endogenous* (caused from within) and *exogenous* (caused by external factors). And I wonder which is worse: the external crisis of not having enough money for rent or to feed your children, or the internal sense that your brain is incapable of attenuating life's daily tragedies. The world is almost always a shitty place, and sometimes it takes a Herculean effort to carry on. I think I've earned my illnesses and my issues.

MY CLAVICLE

Is it naive to think that my pain has an ideological origin? To believe that pain, whether of the body or of the soul, might be caused by a socioeconomic crisis? It's a simple question. I decide, whether naive or not, that yes, ideology is a factor. I pull out my capitalist scale to weigh my pain. If it is physical in origin, the scale tips toward: pharmaceutical industries, private versus slower public health care, physiotherapy sessions, orthopedic devices, analgesics, and the luxury of a healthy diet and lifestyle. If its source is my soul, the scale tips the other way toward: psychologist's notes, psychiatric meds, aromatherapy, yoga, herbal tea, high-end running gear, expensive vacations, maybe a cruise. The scale balances perfectly, measuring both sides as equal, and I realize that I am ideologically lost.

I decide that I will refuse to be a shut-in. I overcome my supposed agoraphobia and go out to see people, but all the conversations end up on the same topic: my condition. I have no idea if exposing my personal health details is a good thing or just helps lock me into a vicious cycle. As I ponder this, I discover that almost everyone I know has had a similar experience: Juan, Nuria, Verónica, José, Mercedes, Mabel . . . I do the math and it adds up to more women than men. Coincidence? I don't think so. In a crisis, where does the pressure always hit hardest?

MY CLAVICLE

So many of us crazy ladies. Legions. Hordes. Natalia gets pregnant and gives birth to a beautiful little boy. They give her an enema. They press on her belly. They give her an episiotomy; they stitch her up. The usual thing. Then the pain starts, traveling from her groin down her thigh, and, later, partial paralysis of her leg. Natalia goes through a host of different doctors, all of whom discover nothing. "Postpartum depression." "Anxiety." "You ladies aren't very tough." Natalia gets worse and worse. They prescribe sedatives. She doesn't take them because she knows she isn't anxious. She insists that something physical is wrong. One year, two years, three years. Natalia is a good-natured woman who continues to teach her classes at the university, now with a limp. She goes back to the doctor and a miracle happens. They finally admit it: "Something's wrong." Natalia has developed a precancerous condition due to an infection. Her episiotomy incision was stitched up incorrectly, leaving a thread from the bandage inside. The doctors suggest that the infection went undetected because the anti-anxiety medication she was prescribed (but never took) might have masked the symptoms. "You could have died," they tell her. Natalia is as reluctant to take the pills as she was before this diagnosis. She's proud of herself, because many times she was tempted to pop one out of its blister pack and into her mouth. To appease the savage beast of pain. To calm herself. To be obliging. To go with the flow. Natalia has surgery. She's left with an array of ongoing secondary conditions. But she's happy now because it's clear she wasn't crazy, or weak, or wrong. She got pregnant again and has given birth to a little girl.

MY CLAVICLE

Nietzsche wrote that there is no pain as intense as that reported by a well-fed, well-educated young woman of the bourgeoisie. Sort of well educated, anyway. I don't recall whether Nietzsche meant *reported* pain or *felt* pain. The difference is interesting. Is it possible that pain is magnified by the reporting of it? And even more if you're unable to explain it and you start to question whether what can't be explained really exists? Could a sense of impotence that your enormous capital of words is suddenly of no use to you in itself intensify your pain?

So, as I was saying, Nietzsche wrote that there is no pain as intense as that reported by a young woman of the European bourgeoisie. Or *Europeanized* women, like the female protagonists in Edith Wharton and Henry James novels. These women, Nietzsche suggests, were aghast at the sight of a single drop of blood swelling on their white fingertips if they pricked themselves while sewing. And yet, though they hired nannies and governesses if their income allowed, these same women gave birth to the sons of the dominant class. Without anesthesia. Between screams. Without screams. Sometimes they died.

Nietzsche reflected on women's threshold for pain. Despite his rejection of Judeo-Christian conservative morality, his reflections exposed him as a misogynist and firm supporter of submissive chasteness. For women. I might fit perfectly into Nietzsche's hypothesis on pain. I've never wanted to have children because it *hurts*. On the other hand, Mr. Nietzsche should have met Natalia. And probably my friends Silvia and Isabel, too.

MY CLAVICLE

When I was a little girl, my mother always complained: "You and your waterworks." I'd turn on the waterworks if I cut my finger. If a thumbtack stuck in my chin. If I had to get a vaccination or a tetanus shot after cutting my leg on a rusty old wagon (it was blue gray). "It's just a booster, just in case," they consoled me. As if that made the shot hurt any less. The waterworks came on when I scraped my knees on the pavement in the playground at school. When I got a loose tooth and they pulled it out with a string. When I couldn't go number two. When I'd bump into something or fall and see with my own eyes how the veins broke under the skin, turning my flesh purple. When I burned myself on a cigarette or on a hot pan in the kitchen. When bacon grease spat out of the pan and scalded my forearm. When a hangnail bled. When my ears hurt from an infection or my mouth from a cold sore. When an insect bite got irritated. When I was afraid at night. When I was cold.

Today I've decided to turn off the waterworks. Going forward, I'll conceal my pain. Only discuss it if asked. I won't talk about the eagle clawing my chest or the tick sucking at my bones. I'll downplay the pain that meanders up and down, left and right. I've decided to become docile, something that I've never been and never wanted to be. But in the end, I can't do it. Even without the waterworks, everyone can see my pain. And this time, I'm not even trying.

There are writers who swim and writers who run. Men and women writers. I'm a walker. But now when I walk, it feels like I could faint at any moment. I notice how the pressure builds around a very precise spot on my body from which the pain radiates until its origin is blurred. *Reported* pain. I am a barometer of myself. I cut myself on the edges of my own bones. I huff and puff, and in the meantime, embracing the cliché of alcoholic writers—Malcolm Lowry, Duras—I drink more than ever. Excessively. I gulp down a glass of white wine to soothe myself. And then another. And another. But I'm still thirsty. I find relief and calm my nerves. I relax. I lose my fear of death, or at least it doesn't bother me anymore. I start to giggle. My husband's fine with my drinking. He's happy that at least for a while I lose my sorrowful expression. My eyes light up. My husband needs to see me smile.

MY CLAVICLE

At home, I concentrate on identifying the exact spot where it hurts. I'm watching TV, but I see nothing. All I see are my dark inner zones, which I observe through a periscope that rises up out of my forehead to survey the landscape. I dive down underneath my skin, searching. My ailment might be hiding in my musculature, my trachea, my throat, my esophagus, my collarbone. My central nervous system. Then my husband speaks to me, and I snap out of my trance, out of the daydream about my illness and my doubts. His words are almost a reproach: "What were you thinking about?" I don't reply. I'm a very self-absorbed woman. I am definitely sick, but I still don't know with what.

My symptoms have flared up. Is it because I'm working too much or because I'm trying to take it a bit easier? I wish I knew. I always used to get sick—the flu, a touch of bronchitis—just as I was going on vacation. Rest seemed to relax my muscles and weaken my defenses. And now I wonder: Is this surge in symptoms the result of my flagging ability to work, or the cause? Yes, I enjoy my work, but thinking of it as fun might not be healthy. It's also required to earn a living, pay the medical bills, and reach a dignified old age. Work deadens the pain.

MY CLAVICLE

I prep for my pulmonary function test. One of my three or four GPs (I've already lost count), the one who looks like he's made of plastic, advises, "Blow up some balloons." It's to expand my lung capacity, he explains. "Blow up some balloons," he says. "If you don't do it, the six seconds of blowing for the test will feel like the longest six seconds of your life." I leave his office terrified. As always, my husband is with me, and he's furious about the things they said to me. He would much prefer they tell me I'm stressed because I travel too much and work too much; he'd prefer that they realize I'm a hypersensitive woman. They should keep to themselves their insinuations of possible illness that start my brain spinning. "The doctor told me to blow up balloons," I say to my husband. He goes to the dollar store and buys several packages of multicolored balloons. Sometimes I struggle to inflate them. Other times, after just a few big puffs, they're full before I know it. I breathe in deeply, stretching my lungs till they hurt, pulling like a badly healed scar, and then I breathe out, counting as I go: *One, two, three* . . . All the way to six. Very slowly.

Little by little, my home starts to look like one of those places for children's birthday parties. A ball pit.

Which would be worse: learning that this jabbing pain, this unrelenting burden, is permanent, or worrying that it will disappear but then suddenly return? It scares me that I don't know. What if it turns out to be a symptom of something darker? A twisted, morbid mess? Or, worse, a symptom of nothing at all? The most dangerous scenario. Inexplicable.

MY CLAVICLE

As I write the word *jab*—which describes the pain in my jugular notch, that concave space Ralph Fiennes's character poetically calls "Almásy's Bosphorus" as his fingertip lovingly traces the dip between Kristin Scott Thomas's graceful clavicle bones in *The English Patient* (Look up the video clip. Worth it!)—as I write *jab*, I remember that tomorrow my physiotherapist will jab three hot needles into my subclavius muscle. To alleviate the pain, of course. The strangest part is that I accept it all with a smile.

There is photographic proof of this. But this time I'm not sharing it.

If you ask me, it's a milquetoast world we live in these days, which I say even as I myself grow increasingly foolish and diminished. Our wishy-washy world loves pink-covered notebooks and cat videos on YouTube. Meanwhile, truly sensitive natures—mine, I can say without false modesty—get unfairly pegged as unhealthy, unscrupulous, or belligerent. Despite that, this unmasking of myself in this text is the best of what I have to give. With it, I acknowledge that it is external stimuli, not an endogenous chemical predisposition, that causes my fear of madness. External stimuli that leave deep cuts, and scars like the shadows of a fractured bone visible in X-rays. Scars in hidden parts of a soul that I don't believe exists. As singing cat videos accumulate likes on YouTube—*Hail, Caesar, those who are about to die salute you*—in the real world people throw rocks at cats perched on fences howling in the throes of heat. These purgative words are the best of what I have to give. I don't do mythical islands, unicorns, or dancing dwarfs. Nor can I write for you a novel about organ trafficking, spy conspiracies, depictions of one fornication after the other, or stories about children who suddenly, in an epiphany, discover the world's pain or its goodness à la Harper Lee. All these fictions just sound like lies to me these days. So the best of myself is to give you these pages where I tell you bluntly that no one really likes cats, and that soon they'll become a plague like pigeons and crocodiles in the sewers of New York City. The world does us a terrible disservice with its smiley faces. True grief, true sensitivity—that is to say, with no false modesty, mine—either gets "fixed" with meds or is punished because it's seen as a weakness or being spoiled, or cruel, or brutal. My cruelty, even. My desire to hurt myself with my thoughts (so I can write about it?) and along the way to hurt others, offending their peace and health as runners, swimmers, or walkers, as parochial fanatics in the battle against botulism and cholesterol. And suddenly, I don't know why—actually, I do know why, but I'm writing that I don't know for literary effect—Jessica Lange comes to mind and her performance in the movie *Frances* in nineteen eighty-something. I could be more exact—these days we all could—but I resist the urge to consult Google. The lobotomy that was performed on Frances comes to mind, and combining the words *mind* and *lobotomy* in the same sentence is terribly unfortunate but in no way an accident. What they did to Frances was a political lobotomy. And with that, I will shut up, because with those two words united in the same fragment of language, I've summarized my tears and the pain in my clavicle, which by now has reached the subclavian artery, and could reach to infinity and beyond.

I pose a question to one of my three or four GPs. Today's GP has a mustache and seems very traditional. He doesn't look like someone who's very fit, and that gives me confidence. He inspires sympathy. The previous ones include a Palestinian doctor who prescribed Lexatin and a doctor who observed me closely, spoke very quietly, and took good care of me, even though I couldn't help thinking he was a psychopath. His fingers were manicured and paraffined smooth. Having passed through so many different hands is by now a bigger problem than my pathologies, whether real or imagined. I suspect a conspiracy to get me to switch to private health care. I'm at a very difficult age. I'm a hypersensitive woman, after all. I ask my third (or is it fourth?) GP, "What will happen when the pulmonologist, the cardiologist, the rheumatologist, and the gynecologist all pronounce me healthy? When they decide nothing is wrong, but it still hurts?" He goes all professional on me: "You might have a respiratory insufficiency." Adding: "Mitral valve stenosis." For a moment, I really want to have respiratory insufficiency or mitral valve stenosis. I really want to find a reason. I push back: "But what if it's not that?" The doctor smiles: "Then you will have to take three pills instead of just one." That was one of the most terrifying days so far.

MY CLAVICLE

I'm forty-eight years old. Not really. I'm actually forty-seven. Two years ago I stopped menstruating. I am a successful woman full of sadness. I'm afraid my parents are going to die. My husband's unemployed. I work nonstop. I don't want to end up alone. I've been very lucky. I've been very loved. I don't know how to be a winner—or a loser. All this happiness, so much privilege—it's frightening to think I won't have enough time to enjoy it.

I describe to the umpteenth doctor the exact location of my jabbing pain: an inexplicable space right between the sternum and the throat. The doctor says, "That's impossible." I point insistently to a hollow spot. I draw circles around it with my index finger. I doodle around it. It's a blank space. The only area of my body where there is absolutely nothing, and all the flesh is ether and archangels. The doctor gets a bit carried away: "If someone were to hammer a nail in that exact spot, it would go straight through to the other side, clean as a whistle." I start to imagine this doctor as one of those magicians who saws boxes in half with young women inside them. I wiggle my toes, like those girls do when the magician separates the two halves of the box. I don't believe in illusionists, and I don't believe in this doctor. I edge away from him. He steps back because he doesn't believe in me, either.

MY CLAVICLE

I write book reviews for an important daily newspaper. I read other people's books and I learn things. Sometimes, like all readers, I start to identify myself with something or someone in the story, despite being a professional reviewer. I recently read an interview with the Argentine poet Fabián Casas. I like what he has to say. He tells a story about a time in his life when he suffered from deep depression. His friend the Argentine poet Ricardo Zelarayán offered a diagnosis: "You've got the horla," like the protagonist of the Guy de Maupassant short story of the same name, who believes that an invisible presence, a horla, is kneeling on his chest, sucking out his life force as he sleeps. Or maybe it's an alien, or a domestic Cthulhu, H. P. Lovecraft's fictionalized cosmic entity. I swear there are times I would love to be Argentine like Zelarayán and Casas. In Spain, we affectionately consider Argentines a people who've read a lot of literary theology, who think that theory is the same as literature, and who are very adept at psychoanalyzing themselves. I would love to be Argentine so I could call my condition a horla and then psychoanalyze myself. And then I'd get better. Or much, much worse.

My friend Marta suffers from an anal fissure. She's thirty-eight and depressed. Her two daughters want her to play with them, but she can't. She suddenly feels very old, and every day is like the myth of Sisyphus: the torment of evacuating her bowels, washing herself, sitting on pillows, lying down, getting up, slowly recovering, feeling relatively good for a while before bed, going to bed, getting up, starting all over again. Marta shows her husband where it hurts, but he doesn't see anything. The position is ridiculous and humiliating. She insists he keep looking, and he makes every effort to investigate, like a proper proctologist. "I don't see anything." She persists: "No, no, no. Not there. You have to look farther inside, more to the right." He still can't see. She starts to cry. She feels alone, as if she's lying or exaggerating. But she's in real pain and doesn't feel like pretending to be strong. She resumes her abject position. "Keep looking," she tells her husband.

MY CLAVICLE

People who put pink covers on their notebooks and press the like button on YouTube videos of cats and beautiful sunrises made even more beautiful, if possible, by the uplifting words of Rabindranath Tagore, Lobsang Rampa, Khalil Gibran, Bertín Osborne; random people who write philanthropical blog posts or dieting advice—these people must have very thick skins to survive in the social media marketplace of brutal comments and insults. Myself, I just can't stomach that sort of bile, even though some might think I'm cruel and brutish. For example, I feel terribly sad watching the wild birds that sneak under the Terminal 1 canopy roof at the airport. They're looking for food scraps in the cafeteria's trash bins, and as I watch them, I can't help hoping they'll be able to nourish themselves with a granule of instant decaf. But then they'll die anyway, trapped inside here, unable to find a way out. My heart aches for them, even as the other passengers watch them and say, "Bold little things!" "How cute!" "Isn't nature amazing?" Then they take pictures with their phones and post them on Instagram.

In the airport my husband says goodbye, and when he confesses, "I'm really going to miss you," I burst into tears. I'm ashamed to see myself in this state, which is a denial of who I really am, or who I think I really am. I'm ashamed of my tears because they are only *relatively* mine, because I am, essentially, a powerful woman, and this display of vulnerability, which represents only a tiny part of my being, leaves my husband very worried. Later, I convince myself that it's not my fault. It's his fault for saying things like that to me. I'm not like that. When the plane lands, I allow my mind to clear. My arms swing rhythmically. I carry my own suitcase. Go into robot mode. Smile and sail through passport control, no matter what country I'm in. Then find a taxi or get on a bus. Change money. Check into my hotel. Connect to the Wi-Fi. That's who I am. Other times, when I travel overseas, I feel almost certain I could die from shyness. Someone could stick a knife in my gut, and I'd be too embarrassed to scream. Then my murderer slashes me, and I bleed out like a lamb for the kebab.

MY CLAVICLE

In a hotel in Monterrey, I sob while watching *Up* on the Disney Channel. I've been told not to go out alone because the city can be very dangerous. Last night the other writers and I went to a cantina to listen to some narco-corrido drug ballads. Dancing was banned to keep fights from breaking out, because everyone knows that men get jealous, and women are provocative, and it all ends up in a fistfight, as one of the waiters explained to us. Now I watch *Up* a second time and I cry for the chubby little Boy Scout. I can hear myself: "I want to go home." I snuffle my snotty nose and feel like I'm three years old. Or 250. I don't know if my feelings are normal, if this kind of catharsis is normal—the passion, the loneliness, the nervousness while traveling, the sensation of being trapped. I don't know if this catharsis is a sign of love and good health or if I should seek professional help. When the movie is over, I read the autobiography of the neurosurgeon Henry Marsh, who writes about the problem of phantom pain. Phantom pain is when someone who has lost a limb, or a toe, or an eye, still feels pain in the missing appendage. I think of distance and the possibility of heartbreak.

El 29/01/2015, marta <msanz@hotmail.com> escribió:
Darling, everything is phenomenal. Excellent breakfast in an amazing cloister. Marvelous hotel. I'm going to a photography exhibit and then for a walk around Cartagena. I love you very much. M

El 29/01/2015, marta <msanz@hotmail.com> escribió:
Hello, my love. I watched the cholesterol at lunch and then pigged out Colombian style at dinner: butifarra sausages, fried green plantains with cheese, fried cornmeal arepas, and fish rolls. The city is very lively and charming. Some friends invited me to dinner, so I invited them over to the hotel for drinks. The margaritas: phenomenal. Tomorrow I'll go for a dip in the pool. Say hello to my folks for me. Big kiss. How is Cala?

El 29/01/2015, marta <msanz@hotmail.com> escribió:
Gorgeous walk through the city with friends. Margaritas and beers. Lovely. But I'm afraid the bill is going to scare you shitless. Missing you here, now, in the hotel.

El 30/01/2015, José María San José <chemasanj@gmail.com> escribió:
I'm so glad, that's all really good. Cala is in heat, yowling up a storm, but otherwise good. Everyone was asking about you at David's event yesterday: Belén, David, José, Edurne, Begoña

from the bookshop, Natalia. Everything's great here. We all miss you, as we always do. Don't hold back on anything; melt that credit card! Try to get some sleep. José told me that the breakfasts at the hotel are amazing. Have fun. Love and big kisses.

El 30/01/2015, marta <msanz@hotmail.com> escribió:
The crows in Cartagena steal fruit from the breakfast buffet. Absolutely everything here is so very García Márquez–ish, it makes me suspect he didn't really exist. The patios inside the houses, the vegetation, the friendliness, everything is eye-opening. The socializing is tiring. But when I go for a dip in the pool and then have breakfast with my macaws, I feel like a total milady. They call me "ma'am" here. I'm about to head out for a walk to enjoy a bit more of the city. It's a movie set, so sensual and luminous that I don't give a damn about the cleanliness. And the glamour. I'm feeling really good physically. Not even constipated—must be the fruit. Lots of kisses to all. Especially Mamá since she's not an internaut.

El 30/01/2015, José María San José <chemasanj@gmail.com> escribió:
I'm so glad. You're cute even talking about constipation. Everything is good here. I went to pick up the leftovers from the party at your parents' house. I'll have lunch with them tomorrow and the day after. We miss you so much! I hope all your presentations go well. It's great that you're enjoying yourself so much. Keep it up.

El 30/01/2015, marta <msanz@hotmail.com> escribió:
Just got back from my walk around the city center. All by myself.

No problem. Taverns, small bars, and terrace restaurants everywhere. We could put away a lot of beers here together, you and I. Lots of Venezuelan exiles. A lot of hustle and bustle. Combination of Asian luxury and semi-poverty; the full-on Colombian poverty is on the outskirts of town. And there, all by myself, I'm not going to go.

El 31/01/2015, José María San José <chemasanj@gmail.com> escribió:
Fantastic. Great. Today I'm having lunch with Charo and Ramón. Mackerel! Great about the pool. I hope you slept well. And that your presentations go well. Cala is a bit irritating, but better. I love you so much. Kisses.

El 31/01/2015, marta <msanz@hotmail.com> escribió:
I can report, in this telephonic writing style that really seems to suit me, that I still haven't done the roundtable with Almudena, but I did attend a presentation, and I learned that the small birds of Cartagena are hanging by a thread, and that here on this grand stage, the rich pay to mix and mingle with writers who turn literature into the kind of spectacle that we do not want it to be. This is both tragic and marvelous, or maybe it's just that I have a little worm inside me that won't allow me to be hedonistic, not even in the Caribbean. Literature is respected and applauded here in a bourgeois fashion, and in the conglomerate of the bourgeoisie there are bad people and there are very good people. We all feel like we're very good and very clever, but there are barriers you never get through, because even if you do, they'll kick you out, and of course, who wouldn't want to enjoy the pools, the bougainvillea, and the Caribbean sea

bass? At the same time, it gives me goose bumps to see how many people come to listen and to learn. How many people still believe in possibly spurious literature. For my part, I'm not going to argue.

With love to you all,
Marta Hamlet Berbiquí

El 31/01/2015, José María San José <chemasanj@gmail.com> escribió:
What you're telling me doesn't surprise you, I'm sure. So, enjoy yourself and don't argue with any of it, *of course*. The mackerel was great, by the way. Stick with the good folks and enjoy that paradise. I love you and I miss you, my darling.

El 31/01/2015, marta <*msanz@hotmail.com*> escribió:
Power failure! Just what I need: alone at night in my room, toothbrush in my mouth, and the lights go out. Up until then, a fantastic day: the roundtable with Almudena went well, but when it came time to sign books, she had a line out the door and I had three blind mice, which is logical for lots of reasons but also because I only had one book, *Un buen detective.* Then the poetry reading was surreal: I antagonized an old Dadaist poet—I think he gave me the evil eye—but earned the respect of a contemporary Colombian writer. I was going to go to a party, but then I ended up staying in the hotel drinking beer and eating cheese with friends (the cheese did not go down so well). Monday afternoon, I'll call Chari to let her know the details of my arrival in Bogotá. Gotta go, the power is still out. I'll pull the blankets up over my head.

Kisses for everyone. It's hard to be away from you.

El 01/02/2015, marta <msanz@hotmail.com> escribió:
Receiving you all loud and clear. I'm going to do a few laps before breakfast. Yesterday a nun wanted to take a picture with me. This is the first time I've had my picture taken with a nun. I'll keep in touch. This Wi-Fi stuff and writing letters to you on a phone is magical. I love you more. M

El 01/02/2015, marta <msanz@hotmail.com> escribió:
I am a Spanish woman writer of indeterminant class who has to stand on tiptoe to see anything and fakes objectivity in order to fit in. It's amazing how much I'm learning and the friends that I'm making, but I had lunch alone in the hotel today because I'm tired of all the socializing.

    Chema, did my critique of Seumas O'Kelly come out in *Babelia* yesterday? How I love you!

El 01/02/2015, José María San José <chemasanj@gmail.com> escribió:
Yes, it came out on Friday. I feel better after talking to you on the phone. I love you.

El 02/02/2015, marta <msanz@hotmail.com> escribió:
I'm in the airport waiting to go to Bogotá. I managed to suck down two hundred euros' worth of beer in the hotel. Martita, the tipsy chick.

El 02/02/2015, José María San José <chemasanj@gmail.com> escribió:
My Martita, living life to the fullest. Have a good flight.

El 02/02/2015, marta <msanz@hotmail.com> escribió:
In my Bogotá hotel. And will carry on with my spending spree. There's no other choice. The cost of meals isn't included here, or taxis or museums. Fingers crossed I don't get altitude sickness. I'm coming from sea level, and here we're very high up. Much, much, much love, goddammit!

El 02/02/2015, José María San José <chemasanj@gmail.com> escribió:
I'm sure the altitude won't bother you. Have fun and do not miss out on anything! Big fat kisses, my darling.

El 02/02/2015, marta <msanz@hotmail.com> escribió:
Soroche—that's what the altitude sickness is called. And no chikungunya fever, not yet at least. But the danger is passing.

El 03/02/2015, marta <msanz@hotmail.com> escribió:
How can I describe this to you? It's an incredible city. Redbrick London homes set amid towering mountain ranges. The restaurant where we ate dinner was amazing. Prawns. Salmon. Grouper. Margaritas. The embassy picked up the tab. The Candelaria neighborhood is magnificent. Tomorrow I'm going to go to the Museum of Gold, the Botero Museum, and the library and then walk around downtown some more, because the city is enormous and awe inspiring. Vibrant. The roundtable talk went well. Almudena sold one book. I didn't sell any. There aren't many of those Cartagena big spenders here in Bogotá. I had no idea this place was so fascinating. The Fondo de Cultura Económica bookstore is amazing. The mountains. Monserrate. The streets. Tomorrow, I'll tell you more. Let's see how I do with my *Amour*

fou presentation. After that there's a black-tie reception with the ambassador. We have to come back here together.

And no sign of altitude sickness.

El 03/02/2015, José María San José <chemasanj@gmail.com> escribió:
Good morning, sweetheart. I knew the altitude wouldn't bother you. I'm so happy you're enjoying yourself so much. And I know your presentation of *Amour fou* will be fantastic, too. No doubts. A thousand kisses.

El 03/02/2015, marta <msanz@hotmail.com> escribió:
I spent the whole morning walking with Marina, a wonderful young woman from the embassy who's like my fairy godmother. Amazing. I'll tell you more about it when I get home, and I can show you the pictures. I've probably taken three hundred already. Crazy. Tomorrow I'm meeting a former student. I ate a bowl of ajiaco. I'm not going to explain what that is. Don't want to scare you.

I miss you so much I can hardly stand it.

I'm going to bed. It's been a very intense day. The book presentation was so-so. I sold four books, and the woman who was supposed to come get me said she got in a traffic accident, which no one believes. Probably not even her. Juan and Luciana send kisses. The ambassador practically starved us to death during his reception, and in the end, we had to go find a pizza place. That was fun, zipping around town in a taxi like a feisty local. A rich one. But enough is enough now, and I only want to get back home to you. Let my folks know what I'm up to. I hope Cala has stopped yowling *Aida* at you. Many kisses.

MY CLAVICLE

Contemporary communication combines neo-epistolary literature with the imbecilic exhibitionism of the internet. We write constantly, desperate to be read. Imbeciles among the imbeciles. Human beings—all of us—have a stupid sort of intimacy. We're not fooling anyone. The emails between myself and my family say what they superficially say—food, literature, the great outdoors, work, money, sleep, shit, health, absence—expressed with a certain enthusiasm. But they also reveal what isn't said. Anyway, that's enough of my dissembling, because, as much as I was enjoying myself, at that point I just wanted to go home.

I know that every time I turn on my computer and navigate the internet—bookstores, Wikipedia, news sites, pathetic Google searches of my own name—someone is watching me. They scare me, these little windows of publicity that already know what I need: books over athletic wear, Marguerite Duras over Raymond Carver. They know almost everything about me, even though I work discreetly and unseen. If I show myself in the light of day they clamp an ankle monitor on my leg, like tracking a seagull. Surreptitiously. I hadn't noticed this before, but I have an orange ring around the ankle of my webbed foot. They can watch me if they want, but my peccadilloes, if any, will always be more innocent than their digital prison.

These days when I travel and everyone thinks I'm this incredibly lucky woman, which I encourage in a way by asking people to invite me to the most exotic and stunning places—Brazil, the Philippines, China, Syria, and Algeria—I notice that a ragged thread hangs from my clavicle. My tick tugs at it, leaving a hole that grows bigger and bigger, creating a void.

Before I leave on a trip, my mother asks me, "Did you pack your umbrella? Insect repellent? Hemorrhoidal cream?" I've got the whole medicine cabinet in my bag, with laxatives and lorazepam. My most recent GP told me I can take three a day. "And if you start to feel really anxious, just put one under your tongue," she says. I won't. I'm never anxious. And also, my GP has the face of a madwoman. Before I leave on a trip, my husband says, "Are you sure you have the right currency?" And then I get mad, with a boundless kind of fury, because I suddenly have the impression that he doesn't know me in the slightest. "You're kidding, right?" I say. My expression probably contains both disdain and self-pity. "Sorry," he says. I don't know how I dare take a step outside the house after these sorts of interrogations. They sabotage me. It's going to be a long flight. When I arrive, I'll somehow have to exchange euros for some local currency—but will it be the right one? I'll somehow have to get a taxi, give the driver the address to the hotel, even ask for a receipt.

In Spanish, in English, in Italian. In any number of languages that I will never speak. But then I actually arrive, get to my destination, and I resolve each problem with an ease and efficiency that surprises even me. I imagine myself a heroine. Maybe I am.

A few proparoxytones never hurt anyone, right? In Spanish we call them "esdrújulas," words whose stress falls on the third-to-last syllable, like *cla-ví-cu-la.* My friend Aurelio collects these words and organizes them into a fascinating list. Some of us just love words. It's possible our fascination is an irritant to certain folks. But how could such a beautiful word ever cause anyone any pain? *Clavícula.* Clavicle. Clavichord. Cleave. Clever. Key.

MY CLAVICLE

I watch a game show that poses a series of multiple-choice questions, and one in particular really worries me. "The clavicle is in the shape of one, a V, or two, an S." I choose the first answer, V, and I'm wrong. There are a lot of reasons to feel embarrassed by this error, but I realize that I've always failed these multiple-choice questions. Not the easy questions, just the ones that matter most to me, that I may be overthinking. However, if you do think about it, the letter *V* is the one that's more likely to jab you.

The source of the pain settles into a single, definitive spot: the terminus of the right clavicle in my jugular notch, my Almásy's Bosphorus. From there, the pain migrates, sometimes radiating up toward my ear or my mandible. Which leads to a diagnosis that's a bit of a shock. The enormous root of a wisdom tooth that doesn't quite emerge is making me grind my teeth, causing pain in what should be a particularly sexy part of a woman's profile. The root of this molar pushes against my thorax and twists it. The pain accentuates my body's imbalance, though imbalance exists inherently in all bodies, even those extremely harmonic and eurhythmic bodies so publicly displayed on the international catwalks and in beauty pageants. I feel like I can't swallow. I feel like a strange object is blocking the eustachian tubes connecting my ears and my sinus cavities, and inside my body a connection is being created between the eustachian and the fallopian. I see my pain in the shape of an oboe or the magnificent tusk of a white elephant. Other days my pain extends down into the pit of my stomach, and my mouth tastes like crushed ants and turtle soup. I think I might have acid reflux, but I'm not sure. It's more like a sensation of emptiness. New tips and diagnoses are collected from new friends. "You should go to a chiropractor." "Get an endoscopy." "Fibromyalgia." I write it all down in my notebook so I don't forget even a word.

MY CLAVICLE

My cousin Chari has fibromyalgia. Fibromyalgia is a mysterious condition that affects mostly women. It's associated with other mysterious conditions like endometriosis and rare types of celiac disease, like lupus with its dark and predatory name. Lupus affects many more women than men. The singer Seal has it, and on him, the facial scars that resemble a butterfly mask seem like a carnival costume, a tattoo, a glamourous ex libris. Chari also has lupus. She was the one who figured out what was going on, because no one else could come up with a plausible explanation for the cysts that were appearing on her arms. It was unthinkable, but even that which can't be thought can happen. Now she has to carefully monitor what medications she takes because they could cause blindness. She's very brave and has had two children. Another condition that mostly women get is costochondritis, which is often associated with certain respiratory issues. We women suffer from mysterious ailments, ailments considered borderline psychosomatic, the neurological affecting the muscular, because we are more sensitive to sound and disruption, and we resist change in our lives. Harsh neoliberal economic policy creates anxiety, and without realizing it, we resist by somatizing it, making it physical. Sleep disorders, stiffness in the bones and muscles, lack of sexual appetite, inflammation of the vulva, anxiety, depression, hypersensitivity in certain areas of the body: these are the kinds of things that prevent Chari from living her normal life.

Fibromyalgia appears to have its origin in disorders that trigger sleeplessness, which in turn is one of its symptoms. At a book presentation by my sociologist friend, I discover that the need to sleep for eight hours uninterrupted is a capitalist imperative to reinforce worker productivity. The sociologist affirms that no one sleeps eight hours at a stretch every day, and to turn this inherent human characteristic into a deficiency, a pathology—to medicalize it—is just another subterfuge in this strange world that we all believe is normal. That's why, the sociologist explains, using behavioral methods with scary messages to get kids to sleep is a form of violence. "Rock-a-bye baby, on the treetop, / When the wind blows, the cradle will rock, / When the bough breaks, the cradle will fall . . ." However, what's normal, what's natural, what's anthropologically logical, is not sleeping eight comatose hours, because if humans had done this through history we would have disappeared as a species. Alert, long-fanged predators would have snacked on us. I know this theory, I explain it and disseminate it, but today listening to him hold forth, I am, first, grateful and, second, wishing I could believe it. That is to say, I can't believe it. My insomnia has little to do with my survival instinct. A fibromyalgia diagnosis makes more sense to me.

After meeting Chari, I decide for the first time to go online and look up my symptoms, which seem to coincide with hers. At first, I'm calm about it. Then I go into a tailspin, spiraling from the tick at my clavicle to cancer of the larynx. And then my husband says, "Stop." And I stop, but I can't help remembering that I have sores in my mouth, that sometimes my gums bleed, that I've lost a lot of weight, and that on occasion my mother has sniffed my breath and said, "Yuck. Doesn't smell so great today." Between fear and death, I choose fear. Fibromyalgia is a disorder that today fits me like a glove. It suits me.

I notice that my husband watches me while I write, which may be affecting what I write and how I write. What I emphasize and what I decide to keep to myself. How fast I type and how long I pause between thoughts. Maybe it's good that he's keeping an eye on me, because I seem to be saying things that I'm not supposed to. The even-tempered woman I used to be just loses it and lets her rage boil over. Or leaves the house with no clothes on.

Ever since that day of my uncontrolled sobbing, my husband doesn't take his eyes off me. Sometimes I catch him peeking through the doorway. Sometimes if I take too long to come out of the bathroom or do anything out of the strict routine—go out onto the balcony, flop down on the bed, rub my temples—he'll ask, "What are you doing?" It's annoying, and sometimes I don't answer, but if he didn't ask, I think it would bother me even more, and I might start to slightly exaggerate my unusual movements and unexpected gestures.

"Are you asleep?"

Back when he was working and had to get up at six in the morning, my husband would fall asleep as soon as his head hit the pillow. I always tell this anecdote that illustrates my perversity: We had just gone to bed, and he fell instantly asleep; envious, I nudged him awake after five minutes, saying that his alarm had gone off and he was late. He panicked, went into the bathroom, took a piss—which he'd done just five minutes before—and turned on the tap in the shower, all before I could bring him back from this deceptive awakening, admitting that in fact it was only midnight. He came back to bed completely happy.

These days, my husband never falls asleep before I do. Sometimes neither of us sleeps because we're each waiting for the other. He's waiting for my stillness; I'm waiting for his, that little sigh of sleep-breath, so I can close my eyes with some tranquility. It makes me nervous, how he watches me at night, and provokes me to worry about his health. As I journey through my insomnia, I don't move, I barely take a breath. He watches. He sits up a bit to see me better. It drives me nuts, but it also makes me happy.

It's getting ridiculous. To ward off any bad news, I'm now giving gifts to the doctor—the third, the second, the first, I don't even remember anymore. I give him one of my books, one I'm not even sure I like that much anymore. It's an extra that I keep in a cardboard box along with a bunch of other old books. Maybe I should have given him a book I liked more, maybe even my best novel—something of real personal worth that's difficult for me to part with. I thank the doctor when the test results and diagnosis are not pernicious. My satisfaction is fleeting. If the doctor told me I was dying, I'd probably still thank him, like Raymond Carver did in his poem "What the Doctor Said."

MY CLAVICLE

I'm suffering a process of crystallization. First, my toes, and then, little by little, the tips of my fingers, my hands with their delicate little metacarpals, my wrists and my veins underneath. Blue and red. Lilacs interlaced. I'm crystallizing from the outside in and from my extremities toward my trunk. The terminus of this solidification protocol, this metamorphosis of liquids and desiccation of the organic and fluctuating, is my navel. My navel transformed into an inverse test tube. First my skin crystallizes, then my muscles, and finally my crystallized liver, because of its sharp edges, slices through the fat and the flesh. The crystallized pharynx and alveoli are like mobiles hanging from the ceiling, baubles tinkling in the breeze. And underneath all that, my crystal bones are like those of infants born with brittle bone disease who break if they're touched. Passing through the birth canal snaps their femurs and their noses, and their fontanel—that little soft spot on their heads—rends along the edges and spreads as they grow. My tarsi and metatarsi freeze. My toes are always so cold. My femurs are frozen. My eyeballs, like ice cubes to chill distillates, and my lips, like glass but with humid salivary glands that create shards which slice everything they touch like fine paper cuts. Stinging. A crystal palate can't produce consonant sounds for fear of a fracture. My crystallized mouth tastes like blood coagulated in a vial.

My chest crystallizes, and through the transparency, I watch the beating of my blue heart. The crystallized scars look like streams of water in a photograph. Crystal braids. My elbows crystallize and the joints poke my musculature, which is getting weaker as each second passes. My nipples crystallize and I am cold. A bout of shivers threatens to shatter me. I mustn't bump into anything, like someone whose skin has been scalded. I separate my legs. My crystallized neck reveals the presence of ganglia, oval-shaped strings of nerve cells that are the beads of a necklace. I am my glass. Fragile. *Don't touch*. I'll sleep in a box full of white Styrofoam peanuts. I am my snow. Crystallizing myself. I am my autoimmune disease. My lupus. I crystallize on my own, but also because of the effects of your care, dear reader. Left alone, that which is beautiful breaks. Though I'm not beautiful, just breakable. I'll step carefully off the curb. In fact, I won't leave the house, in case some child throws a rock and shatters me. In case a gust of wind or a shove destabilizes me. I'm a Lladró figurine, let's say an orchid.

What if this reaction in my body is actually a warning about someone else's illness? What if my process of crystallization is an omen and presages a loss? What if the Dadaist poet in Colombia really did curse me and ascertained exactly what would hurt me the most?

Recently, everyone's been telling my husband, "You look thinner." I hadn't noticed, but now I observe him more carefully. I wake up glued to his side. I smell his odorless skin. I caress his face. I tickle his nipples while he brushes his teeth. No, I don't even want to think about it.

MY CLAVICLE

My friends take good care of me. Luis tells me how lucky I am to have such a loving, attentive husband. All this attention is embarrassing. Still, I like the idea that my friends are talking about me. I like to imagine them worrying.

I am lucky. Luis doesn't know the half of it. My husband goes with me everywhere. He drops me off and he picks me up. He tries to find cures. Physiotherapy, special pillows, doctors who are friends of friends, appointments with the National Health System, emergencies, placebos from our philanthropic pharmacy, tryptophan and sedatives, calming herbs—and if he can't find them, he contrives them. He's constantly on the go. And he does all the housework.

I have a student who's a psychotherapist. I never ever look him directly in the eye. Under any circumstances. I think I'm going to flunk him.

My father teases me by suggesting that the worst thing about the pulmonary function test is the huge size of the tube you have to blow through. "You think it's going to be a slender little tube, but actually the opening is more like the size of a toilet paper roll." I'm fine with my father's peculiar form of shock therapy, but my husband doesn't appreciate this type of humor. This is because my husband knows that as soon as we get home, I'm likely to grab a toilet roll, stick it in my mouth, breathe in deeply, and start to blow. *One, two, three . . .*

This illness—which because it still refuses to show up in any tests now seems darker, more carnal, more lacerating—makes me feel for the first time that my father and I inhabit different worlds. My illness is too contemporary, or too bourgeois. Or, on the other hand, it's the tip of the iceberg of my simple, profoundly proletariat, Judeo-Christian nature. Of my strict sense of responsibility, which is not attuned to my father's hedonism. Paradoxically, in his case, hedonism has little to do with gastronomy, unlike contemporary foodies who seem to equate the pleasure of a great meal with the pleasure of a great orgasm. I wonder if my suffering annoys my father because he thinks it has turned me into a victim who has to buy what she needs to be happy, to alleviate her pain. But what I need most urgently is to name what's happening to me and, with the name, feel that I'm part of something. I'm seeking my tribe, my community.

MY CLAVICLE

A few years ago, I'd have wanted to slap a woman like me. *Snap out of it! Don't be ridiculous.* But not anymore. Now I'm just afraid. A little respect, please, for my tick. My pain. Real or imagined. Or both. It throbs. I can feel it. Physically.

I wonder if shame intensifies the stings of pain. The tick is jabbing me in an apparently deserted part of my body. It's embarrassing to be the one asking my parents for help, when the natural order of things dictates that it should be the opposite at this stage in our lives. Why does my voice crack with emotion every time my mother calls me on the phone? Why do I break into tears when they ask me how I'm doing? Why do I tell her the truth and feel even worse? Why don't I have the strength to hide how I feel? Why do I always have to tell her everything, even the smallest of details that I could just as easily keep to myself? "Mamá, I'm getting a sore in my mouth." "Mamá, I had a dream last night that you were sitting on a bale of hay and wore a Cordobés hat to protect against the sun." "Mamá, I have this weird spot on my skin." And instantly we plunge into a litany of potential dermatological horrors. Removal with liquid nitrogen and full UV protection. Freckles that mutate from impish to malignant. Amid all my ongoing corporal and domestic dysfunctions—sometimes the closets fill up with ghostly odors, flies make nests in the air vent—I choose to expose myself to my mother's advice and admonitions. "Mamá?"

Why do I get so furious at my father because he doesn't understand the dimensions of my pain, my sacrifices, when he asks for things that I can't give? Why do I have to shout to explain to him that it's hard for me to get out of bed? To stand up? To think of anything else? To smile? "Can't you see that I can't do it, as hard as I try?" And then after yelling at him, I remember he's a small, elderly man, delicate like a rose petal, and I deeply regret that the tick in my chest seems to feed off my ire. Why am I so petty, why don't I behave like the excellent liar that I am? Why don't I say to myself, *You're a mature woman of almost fifty years. You're an adult. You're old enough to be a grandmother*?

Logic dictates I should be the one to call and check on my mother, to ask about her blood pressure, her chronic insomnia, her latest test results. But my mother's ailments are erased by my own chronicle of pain. Logic also dictates I should be the one to accompany my father to his oncology appointments and encourage him to be hopeful. But it's possible that instead I blame my father for being an antecedent to my own illness. A history of pathology. I should be worried about them, and even though I do worry, I'm the one right now who's shrinking, getting wrinkles; the one who hurts. I am Gollum. I'm the one who rubs my aging process in their faces, while they decline to indulge their own.

Pathetically, I'm the one who feels abandoned when my parents, retirees in their seventies, announce that they're going on vacation. My mother says, "Your husband should be the one taking you to the doctor." My husband is always by my side, and my mother's words are not a reproach to him. What she's done is cut the umbilical cord between us, forcing me to grow up. She's taken a hammer to the glass box that encases me. In my bifocal brain, I'm torn between imagining that my parents don't care about my symptoms and thinking that they care so much that they don't want to make it worse by changing their normal routine. Or they're distancing themselves from me so I won't have to worry about them, and I can wallow in my pain and heal faster. But what if the wallowing is what impedes my healing?

It's summer. July. My mother and I talk on the phone twice a day, every day, for at least seven minutes each time. We would do this even if I wasn't sick.

MY CLAVICLE

"Blow, blow, blow, blow! More! Even more! Harder! No, no, no! Not like that! I know you can blow harder! Try again! Not like that! Take a big breath and blow, blow, blow, blow! Blow harder! Harder!" In the waiting room, my legs tremble. My husband is with me, and he squeezes my hand. He smiles at me as if to say it's all fine. The previous patient finally leaves. She's an elderly woman with dyed-black hair. Her face is pale. She mutters an insult under her breath toward the person who administered her test. Then I hear my name, and I enter.

I turn on the charm for the nurse who's administering the test. I always turn on the charm for someone giving me a test because it helps me create a false sense of security that it will hurt less. She measures my height and weighs me. Five-foot-two. Ninety-nine pounds. "You're very thin." I try to be clever in my reply: "I think I'm just taller than the last time I was here." I approach the machine and confirm that my father exaggerated about the toilet paper roll, but not by much. I take a deep breath, and I blow, blow, blow, blow. You only need to tell me once.

MY CLAVICLE

Five-foot-two. Ninety-nine pounds. "You're very thin," she says. When I started menopause, they ran blood tests and discovered I had moderately high cholesterol. *Dyslipidemia* is the technical term for it, and it represents all the prohibitions that from that moment on have marked my life. I can't eat mayonnaise or cakes or red meat or pasta with chorizo. I can't eat sausage sandwiches or cheese or sea urchin gratin. I can't eat chocolate or shrimp or squid. I can't eat a cheeseburger or ossobuco or steak tartar. I can't eat butter or fried pork rinds or French fries or olives stuffed with tuna. No octopus or pork cheeks or pâté or caviar or sauteed sweetbreads. No bacon and eggs or fabada stew. No crispy cheese snacks or ice cream. My mother has to skim all the fat off the top of her stew four times before I can eat it.

I can eat turkey, skinless chicken, vegetables, fruits, legumes, all kinds of seafood as long as it isn't breaded and fried. I can eat sushi and sashimi. Soy sprouts, bread, and pasta as long as it's not egg pasta. I can drink herbal tea, skim milk, water, and lots of liquids, all in order to lower my cholesterol level by 10 percent. I can eat air and dance like the ballerinas of *Les sylphides*.

I walk about an hour each day. I go to the gym. I sweat. I'm consumed with guilt when I break any of my healthy habits. And I do break them constantly, or at least it seems like I do. At the same time,

I worry that my rigid diet will alter the way I think. Not due to hunger or lack of nutrition, but to the Stakhanovite effect.

Sometimes I imagine that my pain didn't begin in that uncomfortable seat—17C—of an airplane flying across the Atlantic as I was reading Lillian Hellman's memoir. Nothing could really be that novelistic and intellectual. Maybe what really caused my pain was grinding my teeth in my sleep and my newfound slimness.

I have an eating disorder brought on by our public health system. Like 90 percent of our population.

MY CLAVICLE

For the second time in my life, I write to purge myself. I have faith in the cathartic effect of writing, all my words a prayer. *Please, please, please.* The first time, it helped me recover from a shitty love affair. This time, I'm not so sure. And I ask myself: Is it fair to hurt others by sharing the fears that nag me like a stone in my shoe? I'm referring to what I'm doing with my family, but also to the exercise of writing itself, what I'm doing right now. It's an extreme sport.

My husband got a job offer. It was to oversee the operation of a machine he's never used. A night shift, working alone. The risk of accidents due to his inexperience was high, and the fact that, in order to keep costs down, he'd be working alone led him to say no. I told him, "They'll never call you again," with a look of resentment on my face. He noticed, and his face sagged. Later I felt like shit. I apologized, and he started smiling again.

MY CLAVICLE

The cardiac stress test nurse is tall and stocky and speaks with a Canary Islands accent. She highlights her hair, draws cat eyes on her lids with brown eyeliner, and cuts her fingernails short. She wears regulation clogs and a white lab coat, but still manages to look disheveled. A cheap and ugly necklace hangs around her neck. You can barely see her collarbones. I will always remember her. She chugs down mineral water from a liter bottle. She smells like cigarette smoke. She smokes, smokes like a chimney, and that makes me realize that I now belong to that select group of mature individuals who obsess about their vices, their virtues, and their ailments. And it dawns on me that maybe the things that we're moved to talk about are also the things worth writing about. Maybe there's no need to surgically separate everyday themes, like shopping for onions or making a copy of the house keys, from the more literary themes, like the strange and morbid decomposition of Edgar Allan Poe's M. Valdemar. The nurse whom I will never forget smells of blonde leaf tobacco, and now that I've become one of those former smokers who's recovered her sense of smell, I begin to judge others like her, dividing humanity into the guilty and not guilty. The nurse who administers my stress test may be guilty of committing suicide by cigarette. But I'm not, not anymore.

In the waiting room everyone's checking out each other's shoes. The older women wear sneakers that have got to be uncomfortable, because I know it's not what they normally wear. Elderly patients should be allowed to come in wearing their slippers. I'm wearing moccasins with the laces loosely tied. They're the shoes I use to run errands around Madrid. The ones that don't cause blisters or deform my feet. Suddenly I'm mortified that they'll turn me away because of the moccasins, but when it's my turn, the stress test nurse glances down toward my feet but makes no objection. "Are you comfortable?" I nod briskly. This kind doesn't tolerate indecision or vacillation. "Okay then." Following protocol, she asks me if I've eaten anything before coming for the test, and I say no and that I don't really understand having to fast for a test that consists of running on a treadmill. I say that I'd understand if it were an endoscopy or a blood test, but for running on a treadmill it seems somewhat counterproductive to fast and I might even faint. Of course, I say, I have a banana in my handbag to gobble down as soon as I'm done. I flash a smile. The nurse looks at me with a touch of disdain: "It's to avoid vomiting." And in a voice brimming with malice: "So you don't choke to death."

The nurse undresses me from the waist up, as if I were a child about to be bathed. She corrects my posture with a hard jab to the kidneys. She adjusts my bra straps. I'm surprised. I stiffen. In my mind, I question whether these apparent concessions to elegance and orthopedics are part of the protocol. But I keep quiet and for an instant forget about myself. The situation intrigues me because now I have something to write about, and also, I never could have adjusted my bra straps with the physiotherapeutic professionalism that this woman has. The loose straps on my purple bra, the ones that always fall off my shoulder all the way down to my elbow and I have to pull up by sticking my hand down awkwardly through the neck of my sweater, are transformed by the nurse's professional manipulation into two pulleys that lift my breasts to a height they haven't reached in a long, long time. "That's better." The nurse speaks with assurance. With satisfaction, even. I take a breath, and the little wings of my scapulae unfold and tremble. I sit up straight. Then I'm no longer her mannequin as her focus turns to populating my chest, arms, temples, and wrists with stick-on electrodes attached to cables. I can't even tell you all the different parts of my body that get wired up. I can't tell if what I'm seeing is my body or a scene from a horror movie.

The stress test nurse confirms that my blood pressure is normal. It's one of the few things that I can brag about, physically speaking, the harmony of my blood pressure. The high and the low in perfect balance: 120 over 60, 110 over 55, 120 over 65. Somewhere around there. A miraculous result that unfortunately, as the stress test nurse points out, is not repeated when it comes to my lipid panel or my friggin' hematocrit test, which measures red blood cells (i.e., oxygen levels) in my blood, but I don't even want to talk about that now because it's so bad. Viscous blood. No oxygen. In response to this hematocrit test shaming by the nurse, I take revenge by acting like one of those classic nonsmoker assholes who used to criticize me, sniffing and wrinkling their noses. "You smoke." She nods, and I attack: "Aren't you afraid to take a test like this one?" The nurse shakes with laughter. "I would never ever take this test." She's trying to scare me. It works. She stops talking, then says with completely feigned courtesy, "Please, this way." I get the feeling that this chain-smoking nurse, skilled adjuster of bra straps, dour Canary Islander with a couple of extra pounds on her hips, would have loved to tack an arch *Your Majesty* to the end of that invitation, but stopped herself to deny me proof of her false courtesy.

The nurse helps me mount the already moving treadmill and places my hands on a bar directly in front of me. I look at her tobacco-stained fingers, and the stench that I have never liked washes over me again. "Hold on tight." I'm afraid of falling, but I don't want to disappoint the stress test nurse, and so I start to run. She lets me run for a few seconds and then says, "You don't have to run." She says a brisk walk is good enough because I'm going to be walking for a good while. "How long?" My mouth is already old gauze. The nurse takes several long pulls on her water bottle, swishes the water around in her mouth, and takes her time answering. "Dunno. Whatever you think." The stress test nurse should never have spoken those words to me, because even if I die on this treadmill, my stubbornness will keep me walking into the night, through dehydration and total desiccation of my internal organs. But this woman, who looks like she'd like to slap me at any moment, she doesn't know me and doesn't realize that I'm capable of walking on this treadmill until my skin flakes off in the wind. "You're doing it all wrong." She says it as though she doesn't care but, at the same time, as if life itself depended on it. "Now, let's see if this machine can finally capture a correct reading." I can tell she wants to say "correct *fucking* reading," but bites her tongue. However, the act of swallowing the swear word—maybe she's trying to quit smoking? going through withdrawal symptoms?—isn't the important thing. The important thing is that my heart starts to pound wildly when it gets the message, loud and clear, that there is still no correct reading.

MY CLAVICLE

The nurse readjusts my posture, giving me another jab to the kidneys. "Hold in your gut, stand up straight, tuck in your rear. Like that. Now." I am martial and mechanical. The nurse sucks on her water. The machine emits indecipherable sounds, and I carry on as if I were all alone. I stare at the treadmill's program screen in front of me. I'm running along the ridge of an endless Andean mountain range. My calves are hard as rock. I have no intention of stopping unless my stomach starts to hurt, because I read somewhere recently that symptoms of a serious illness don't manifest the same in men as in women, that the books are all written by men from their patriarchal perspective, so if I am going to have a heart attack most likely the pain will appear in my stomach and not in my arm. I can smell the intense odor of nicotine on my nurse's skin. I know she's there, even though I'm not looking at her. We love each other. We hate each other. I go on and on. I feel a little bit dizzy, but I continue, I persist. My esophagus burns, and my throat. My guts are churning. My knees are about to give out. Fat drops of sweat create rivulets down my scalp that will leave my hair looking greasy, and I'll seem even uglier and more haggard. "The test is over." I am about to stop when the nurse decides to mess with me. "But you can keep going as long as you want." She says it with malice. And I keep going. I look at her and I keep going. I even speak to her with a mouth that barely seems to exist, because my lips are consuming each other, and my tongue is stuck to my palate. "Keep going." I have to rip my lips apart just to pronounce those two words. I'm hoarse. She chirps something I don't understand. And I carry on ten seconds more. I step off the treadmill with my chin held high. I stand on tiptoe to make myself taller. My nurse is two heads and three bodies taller than I am. "At the end you were doing much better." She looks like she's about to break out laughing. The machine spits out a strip of paper with my stress test results, and she tears it off. Professionally, but not very gently, taking some skin with each one, the nurse rips off the electrodes, each one leaving a whiff of dioxide and cyanide that contaminates the scent of my new after-bath cologne. She briskly readjusts my bra straps. (Only after I get home will I discover one electrode still stuck to my skin, still binding me by electric current to my nurse.) Her brusque movements hurt me, but I don't care. She exits the room through a side door a few seconds before me.

MY CLAVICLE

I could have started this whole book with the chapter I just finished writing. My incident with the stress test nurse. At the end of the line "She exits the room through a side door a few seconds before me," I could have added a question, a gloss for you, dear reader, about what led me to be that patient striding along on the treadmill while a machine records my blood pressure, my heartbeat, and other data points I prefer to ignore. Pressing my head between my hands in a gesture of desperation, I could have thrown questions out to you, sharing with you, asking you point-blank: *How did I get here? By what path? What vicissitudes have led to my decline and my possibly illusory path toward recovery?* These questions would oblige you to fill in a blank, to scratch an itch, to contemplate your own history. The questions might have triggered a mechanism by which the reader becomes intrigued and is caught up in my web of suspense, transforming a story about a medical condition and a ghostly horla into a detective novel. Both the ghost story and the medical reality tale would disappear, disintegrating like a cheap pulp fiction cover soaked by the rain and crushed in a clenched fist.

But that's not what I've done, because the pages of this book are not conceived to be conventionally interesting. They follow a different protocol. They are an investigation, a search. An effort to respond to a question that doesn't necessarily follow a strict chronological order. These pages aspire to drill down, like sharply honed tools. An auger. A bone drill. These pages describe a process, possibly a circular one, and speak of a person. Not her dance moves.

A series of specialists has examined me and given me the all clear. I'm now accumulating encouraging reports. My husband says, "Aren't you happy?" He wants more than anything for me to be happy. But I can't be, because I still don't know the source of this heavy darkness. Later the poor little faces of the bald children come to mind, and despite my pain, I feel like an imposter. Instantly I rebel: I also have the right. To my pain. To my own and perhaps not so frivolous affliction. I feel another stab: the adjective *frivolous* pains me so much I almost burst into tears.

I review our income and expenses these days with apprehension. In the past, when I was younger and ticks didn't embed themselves over my respiratory tract, I didn't care about money. We went through periods much harder than these and I didn't suffer so much anguish. I ignored both income and expenses for so long that now, for me, money—lacking it, to be specific—has turned into a superstition. A fluid and inexorable misfortune. A destiny and a stain. Something you can't control or hold in the palm of your hand.

A girlish pulmonologist suggested baseline anxiety treatment, and a cardiologist with pearl earrings said, "Anxiety doesn't exist. Go to a rheumatologist." My pharmacist recommended osteopathic remedies, sugar pills, vitamins, and placebos. I've been to the physical therapist. I have a referral for a specialist in digestive tracts. I have phone numbers for a couple of psychotherapists. I've been to my gynecologist. It still hurts. My last hope is to hire an exorcist.

My husband encourages me to say no. No, no, no. I say no to things I would have previously said yes to. A trip to Argentina. Another to São José do Rio Preto in São Paulo. He doesn't want me to suffer an intense episode of pain—a little bit of pain would be okay—while I'm alone in a hotel. The tick no longer chokes me but still nudges my chest a little with its claws as if to say, *I'm still here. Watch out. I could come back stronger at any moment.* My husband doesn't want that to happen while I'm on the other side of the planet amid the macaws and the dry martinis; he just wants me to return safely from paradise. He doesn't want anyone taking my picture while I'm choking because, as hard as I try, I can't get enough air into my lungs. We don't want to have to buy the magazine that publishes those photos. I'd probably look like a cadaver.

My husband is afraid of my fear and afraid that I'm fading. He doesn't want me to accept jobs just to keep poverty from the door or to cushion our old age in bubble wrap. "Only do what you truly enjoy." I smile wryly. My husband is not naive, and he follows the news—he can even tell you the current price of a barrel of crude oil—but either he's not paying attention to what's happening around us, or he believes that it shouldn't affect me. I must not be affected by the joblessness, the poverty, the deadly diseases, the hate. My husband locks me up in the glass box that my mother just broke, and I'm grateful to him for it. I'm grateful to both of them for different reasons. Despite the glass walls of my box, my husband doesn't want to stop me from going wherever I want to. If I want to go to Morocco or to Sant Sadurní d'Anoia, or if I'm convinced that I'll be happy in Babia or Sevastopol, he encourages me, and when I go, he sends me messages and waits patiently for me at home. And then when I get back, he tells me what he knows he needs to tell me so I won't get mad: "The house feels strange without you in it. I'm completely at loose ends." I tell him that sounds like someone who misses their cat that just died, which of course pisses him off.

With my husband out of work and me saying no to almost everything while mentally calculating the collapse of our domestic budget, my husband and I get up together in the morning and go to bed together at night at the same time every day. We aren't apart even for a second. Sometimes it's marvelous. Other times it's suffocating, and when he lurks behind me as I write I think we can't go on like this. "Stop reading over my shoulder!" He doesn't really read my stuff while I'm writing, but he does hover, fearful of what I might come up with. In case it hurts us. He knows that I have an exacting sense of authenticity, but he also knows he has the right to read anything I write about him. I spend all my time writing about him, pondering *us* with increasing fervency as the years go by. Before, I didn't think about *us*. Now, *us* is all I think about. I've always believed that overthinking relationships, fiddling with them, marks the beginning of the end, so I surprise myself with my preoccupation. Shock myself, actually. "Stop reading over my shoulder," I insist, but actually that's just an excuse for my lack of concentration, or lack of enthusiasm. Writing surreptitiously excites me. It's both natural and innately naughty, like masturbating when you're too young to really know what you're doing. If I were alone at my desk, I'd review my emails and then check my yogurt supply in the fridge. (Yogurt—I never actually eat it.) My husband is the imaginary man who stalks me. My favorite infantile fantasy. Is he there? Not there? Yes! He's there, and I run. I run away hoping, please, please, he'll catch me. He's behind me, faceless and mute, and I don't have a moment to lose. Suddenly, I feel caught in flagrante, but that's absurd. My lips are sealed.

In the end, yes, I do think it's possible to be together all the time. Because we feel like it, and because during our moments of separation—a breather—we suffocate even more than when we are always together. "Are you okay? Really, are you sure? Is anything wrong?" We're Siamese twins. Storks. Big old monogamous birds. We can't live without each other anymore, even though these days this kind of codependency isn't something you'd really want to publicize. It's not as if I don't know how to be alone. I grew up learning to play alone and hum to myself. To write alone. No, it's not solitude in the abstract, it's about a concrete solitude in which I don't know how to be alone without him.

Every time I say no to a job offer, the tick loosens its grip on my sternum while another, smaller tick—I don't know if it will grow—approaches me timidly and finds a spot. Despite it all, I think I feel a bit better.

MY CLAVICLE

Downer DNA. My pessimism. The evil eye. This is what my otherwise enviable trip to Manila boils down to, and I didn't even travel alone. I publish a poem in *Perro Berde*. It's going to be translated into English. It's all a privilege.

1.
The worst we could have seen we saw as soon as
we left the Manila airport.

A little girl, dirty and half naked, begging for money.

According to our calculations as well-nourished observers
—every Westerner, when traveling, carries in their bag a
      pediatrician, an economist, a televangelist, and a
      gastroenterologist...—,
the girl can't be more than four years old.

Although maybe she's actually nine or ten, and doesn't drink
      milk, but smokes when no one's looking.

If magic and poetry help us digest this scene,
maybe,
the girl is just a little old lady dressed up as a
>	*baby doll,*
in Manila City,
before slipping into the jeepney that takes her to a bordello,
>	or a rotting landfill,
to paint her nails and wait for the tourist
—every Westerner, when traveling, carries in their bag
a pederast, a patriot, a hypochondriac, and a
Minister of God, or of the Interior . . .—;
if magic and poetry help us,
then maybe the little girl is an octogenarian who's had
>	a thousand facelifts and surgeries,
and burned her palms so that
>	no one can identify her
as a recognizable member of the mendicant underworld of
>	Manila.

We ask poetry to help us,
but the girl is a Manila girl
who knocks on our taxi's window, and we
>	see her as a fragile creature
with birdlike bones and the eyes of a lamb.

MY CLAVICLE

On my phone I get a pressing message from Amnesty
        International that I erase
almost as vertiginously as I beg for poetry to help me
        —every Westerner, when traveling, carries in their bag
        a sommelier, a meteorologist, a soccer player, and
        a bard...—,
not to see the little whore girl, little whore girl, little beggar girl of
        Manila City's impoverished underworld,
who holds in her arms a beautiful baby boy with
        a fat, round head.

A crust of gray mucus coats his turgid skin.

The baby balances on the girl's waist, and it seems like she might
        drop him.

We fear hearing the sound of a wineskin crashing onto
        the muddy street,
because every Westerner, when traveling, hides in
        their bag a tuning fork
to differentiate the pure *la* from any other note and
also keeps there an engineer of highways, canals, and ports.

Someone who measures and compares without stopping to
           think why some men's legs are longer than others
or why in Manila the girls look at you with smoke
as they rap their birdlike knuckles on the
           taxi's window.

The worst we could have seen we saw as soon as
we left the Manila airport.

2.
But the little girl and the baby boy with the beautiful, immense head are not just an image to be contemplated. They are flesh and blood intruding in our space within the taxi, and they force us into a sort of painful concentration. The children will remain forever embedded in my eyes. Then we'll look quickly away and pretend to speak to each other, but my husband says, "Now we've seen the most horrible thing there is to see in Manila City."

Meanwhile, I follow the steps of the little girl who, with the little boy balancing on her waist, returns to the awning where a woman waits for them, hanging a tattered canvas between the concrete piles of the bridge. The little girl gestures that we haven't given them anything, and I recall the message on my phone from Amnesty International: "Marta, I'm worried that we are becoming used to it." The woman strikes the child who has returned to the poppy-less concrete of the bridge with her hands empty of dollars or the garish Philippine paper currency. I wonder what the girl's name is, and why Amnesty International has taken the liberty of calling me by my first name. Why are they using these marketing tactics, acting so friendly and affable, obliging me to immediately delete all their petitions. The traffic light holds us in an eternal Manila City traffic jam, and I can see in the rearview mirror the baby boy's splendid fat head resting on the edge of the roadway. Crawling across his little hand is a centipede, or one of those unidentified insects that are born, live, and die in this jungle city of metallic structures and vegetation resistant to CO_2. All these things together constitute the ecosystem of Manila City. My husband says, "Now we have seen the most horrible thing we could have seen." I doubt it, though I wear a face mask with sunscreen that catches bits of carbon from all the motorcycles. The dead insects of Manila City.

3.
Of Quiapo, all I remember are the movies of Brillante
        Mendoza,
the lobbies of cinemas where feral white
        cats lazily sleep,
the polished soles of the Nazarene's feet,
the ointments and the sampaguita jasmine,
the shops with sandals of a thousand colors,
the muddy puddles and billboards
        with smiling middle-aged women wearing
pearl necklaces and perms with sienna-colored hair
        from a box.

We smell the blessed scent of insecticide that will
        exterminate centipedes crawling on infant arms.

In Quiapo
we capture aerial views of the faithful who throng to
        church on Friday afternoons.

They are small dots of green, purple, and red.

Tiny figures wearing oversized cotton shirts.

Voodoo dolls.

Their skin pixelated from up above on the bridge that crosses
        the avenue.

Zombies, little zombie girls, roam among the throng with
        outstretched hands
while holding mandrill-like babies whose fingers clutch
        the girls' thirty-pound bodies.

Children, free or rented, all prematurely dead, scamper
about everywhere and wash their faces with stagnant water
from oily puddles where rain never falls.

4.
"Marta, I'm worried we're getting used to it." I'm engaged in a personal dialogue with Amnesty International, and I respond, "Yes, yes, yes. Absolutely. We are getting much too accustomed to all these saintly, complacent, and repetitive cell phone messages. Also to the sad or offended emoji faces. To not giving money to little girls under the bridge. To discouraging panhandling in the cities. To what I don't see but believe. To what I see but can't believe."

Every Westerner, out on excursion, carries in their suitcase
        and makeup bag:

a publicist, a good man with a guilty conscience, a housekeeper
        who cleans the windows and is about to
            fall and crack open her head on the brick patio.

5.
But we no longer see anything because we are bewitched
        by the colorfulness of the poor,
certain that we have already seen the worst that could be seen
        on landing in Manila City,
the black eggs of the buried bird,
those proteins, that crunch between the teeth,
and the rats that scurry through the gardens of hotels that are
        almost luxurious.

We have broken through invisible walls that are like blasts
        of hot air.

On the other side awaits the coolness of air-conditioning, sushi,
        and Siberian huskies wearing
        crocheted booties

We've already seen it all, and we know that we cannot eat
        the street food.

We aren't vaccinated, but we arrived with our defenses
        raised high,
we wash our hands every fifteen minutes
and we protect ourselves with our sunglasses
        and our sunscreen.

We think we know everything, but maybe the worst and the best
        have escaped us.

In our bag we carry: a pediatrician, a soccer player, a roadway
        engineer, a troubled singer, a little wedge of La Vaca Que
        Ríe *light* cheese, a fellow traveler, a compulsive photographer,
        perfumed wet wipes, and a storyteller.

The newspapers are filled with good news that I'm not sure how to interpret. I'm not talking about GDP rising because of disposable income and new job creation. I'm not talking about those empty phrases in the financial press. What I'm talking about is the invention of a pill that awakens women's sexual desire. Women! We're in luck! Finally we can have sex again. "They" have discovered that not making love—with anyone? at any time?—is actually a pathology, and to be healthy you have to keep having sex right up to the day you die. You have to die making love and loving it, and also working out at the gym, and, of course, stopping to smell the roses along the way. Those ninety-something widows who look around and say, sensibly, "What am I actually still doing here?" Not allowed. They must also still make love and take pills to make love and die full of rage that they have to die. Pharmaceutical companies, the porn industry, lingerie manufacturers, dating sites, the makers of cold gels and hot gels, the makers of ropes and chains and handcuffs, bolero singers, vaginal gel advertisers, and rose growers have conspired against that stoicism that helps us to die. To hell with Zeno of Citium. (Zeno, ancient Greek founder of stoicism. But you knew that.) "They" argue that absence of desire is bad because it paralyzes life, although the truly frightening paralysis is the one that hits your bank account. Desire isn't always a biological compulsion. Lingerie and ointment manufacturers, for example, fabricate it, weave it into an imaginative filigree that repulses me at this moment when I have chosen to spit out the truth.

The desire that I claim is the one that inspires me to write a book or shove the director of a bank that's defaulted. Desire for the weird and offbeat. I abhor desire that's artificially inoculated into a body when that body is preparing to sleep and slowly reach its end. I don't want to function artificially. Salivating, lubricating, slurping artificially. There's a moment in life when it's good not to come anymore. You have to stop coming. I want them to leave me in peace. To allow me to forget about my body. For better or worse. Forget about multiple orgasms, spasms of pleasure that are sometimes more intense, sometimes less, the electrifying jolts and the yearning to repeat them again and again. That form of love and abandon. I want to forget about the possibility of fucking so much and so well that it burns. Forget fingertips, forget Almásy's Bosphorus, forget mandibles, wisdom teeth, and the box that constrains my heart. Forget the advent of tumors and the corrosion of my DNA. I don't want them to sell me anything. I will kill the door-to-door salesman who tries to sell me desire that would only be an emulation. An imposture. A fake. It wouldn't be born from my gut but from a foreign substance that would scramble my synapses and include a long list of side effects—dry mouth, insomnia, irritability—that I would have to battle with even more potions.

I don't know how to interpret the good news in the newspaper: "The IBEX stock exchange nudges up again, rising by 2 percent to 10,200." But I do know that stress is one of the major causes of lack of desire, more than exhaustion, age, boredom, lack of opportunity, laziness, fear, apathy, a need to forget your own body from the inside, aneurisms, the sagging—malignant or benign—of the flesh on my arms. I am the perfect client for the pills they want to sell for everything. Pills because I don't want; pills because I want too much. And now it seems that I must acquire a vibrator or hire a gigolo who can thaw the arctic corners of my body. But I remember discovering masturbation while climbing trees or maybe sliding down a railing, that sensation that was mine only, egotistically fantastically mine, for which at the same time I feared being discovered at fifteen, sixteen, even thirty years old, when the flesh voraciously demanded it, and every little genital twitch engendered guilt. Insults. Sow. Slut. A nymphomaniac whose clitoris is going to stretch out as long as a kief pipe. Back then, when I was young, they probably would have tried to sell me cold showers or tranquilizers. An ecumenical admonition. Fear of infection. In the end, we're never satisfied. Such an injustice.

On a piece of paper, my husband lists my income by month: he repeats the numbers back to me in singsong, like a chant from Latin Mass. Here's what I earn: in January, 1,265 euros; in February, 325; in March, 7,000; in April, 122; in May, 650; in June, 500; in July, 1,450... My husband reassures me: "See? No worries. None at all." But as I gaze out the window at the street below, then across to the horizon, I think no, I don't believe it.

MY CLAVICLE

Even when I don't seek to wallow in these negative thoughts, they mysteriously come to me anyway. I crawl into bed and grab a book—*Dr. Gully's Story*, by Elizabeth Jenkins—flip it open, and read the fictionalized account of a real Victorian doctor who falls in love with a young woman patient he's treating for "hysteria," a condition she's developed because of her husband's brutality. In treating her, Dr. Gully connects the dots. Emotional distress causes physical symptoms, and physical decline feeds emotional distress. In his medical notes, Dr. Gully writes: "Morbid impressions commencing in the brain are reverberated on the visceral ganglionic system, exciting in the viscera sensations and movements. Abnormal sensations and movements in the viscera are reflected in the brain."

It gives me hope to think that if we can truly control our emotions, we might be able to slam the brakes on a pathology, but I don't completely believe it. Something grates on me. Something doesn't fit. Despite that, I abruptly decide that I *must* halt the spinning in my brain if I don't want to end up getting lymphoma. There have already been two cases in my family: one Hodgkin's and one non-Hodgkin's. The second was fatal.

My friend Isabel has had many more procedures than I have. Colonoscopies, laparoscopies, scans of all sorts, and small surgeries. Also, a cystography, where they inject you with a contrast dye that stains the veins of the human bladder and other parts of the urinary tract to expose different ailments. As a young woman, I suffered from chronic cystitis induced by a passionate nature and an athletic approach to sexuality. Then an internist insisted on ordering me a cystography. When he explained to me what the test consisted of, my bladder magically retracted like a snail on a cloudy day, and I never again got cystitis or anything like it. It was then I learned that the body is wary. It takes precautions to protect itself. It won't be bullied so easily.

Isabel's gynecologists have diagnosed her pain as benign cysts and tumors. But she kept complaining because the pain persisted. Then the gynecologists told her she was mistaking the source of her pain. She wrote about it to me in an email: "Then they told me that I was confusing where the pain was coming from and that it really was my urinary or digestive tract." There's resentment in her words, understandably, though the concept of "confusing the source of the pain" is frighteningly plausible to me, even though that feels offensive to the accused. If Isabel lived in Boston or Milwaukee, she couldn't afford so many tests to begin with, but she might be talking to lawyers instead, to sue the gynecologists.

The urologist that Isabel ended up seeing offered a hypothesis, never conclusive, that she might be suffering from endometriosis. Endometriosis is a disorder that takes an average of nine years to be diagnosed. I read about it in a newspaper, and I thought that if my pain—my tick—had lodged near my navel instead of my clavicle, it's completely possible that I'd be thinking about how my endometrium was working. As for Isabel, despite the urologist's hypothesis, which she was very grateful for, her psychologist and her GP opt for a more generalized diagnosis: perimenopause. Meanwhile, Isabel takes pills, cleans the house until it shines, and drinks nonalcoholic beer.

In one of her more recent emails, she writes: "I think about your parents a lot, but it's been a while since I've seen them. I guess we're on different schedules, and I trust they've recovered from the loss of their little dog."

My parents' dog, Cloe, who was adorable, died recently. Now the house feels empty. My mother has a photo of herself holding Cloe in her arms while sipping an aperitif in a bar. I imagine she's sad about the lingering ghost of her dog, but she doesn't want to get another one because she wants to go on a cruise, visit Saint Petersburg, and go to the movies without feeling guilty.

Throughout my ordeal, I've continued my social life, and I've told everyone about the characteristics and intensity of my symptoms. The color of my illness and how it's evolved. So now I have to make amends to all those who've listened to me. I have a guilty conscience about being so tiresome, and now I feel like I need to reassure all my friends. Shut it down. Not talk about it anymore. In other words: lie. I explain my recovery with the aid of mythic narratives, which, like all legends, contain a kernel of truth: the feeling of suffocation was caused by a pulmonary retraction due to an inflammation of the clavicle. The muscle strain was the result of excessive exertion while trying to breathe, thus intensifying the overall pain. My illness has a rheumatic skew, or maybe it's just that doctors should actually be paying more attention to menopause. The Change should not just be about trying to sell us yogurt and adult diapers. I tell my stories, and as I tell them, I convince myself. I notice how hard I work to ensure everyone thinks I've never had an anxiety attack.

Maybe if I conceal my pain, it will go away.

It's my birthday, and my friend Inma calls me. We talk about summer and the heat. I tell her I'm feeling a lot better, then I change the subject because I'm tired of talking about myself, tired of explaining, and especially tired of lying. "And you? How are you?" Inma has anemia, and they've induced menopause so she won't lose iron, and all her energy along with it, through her monthly cycle. She's exhausted. She's had a thousand injections, the kind that hurt like the devil. She's eaten pounds and pounds of liver fillets. Complete garbage. Nothing works. Her hair has lost its curl and hangs limply on her shoulders. "Can you believe it?" she says. Inma has always cared a lot about being beautiful, and now I detect a sad and languishing tone in her voice. It's a wonder her legs even support her. She works in the prosecutor's office and has to visit courts all across Madrid. She waits in lines. She feels obligated to disguise the true depth of her exhaustion out of fear that her colleagues will resent her slowness at work. The doctors endlessly prescribe medication. We talk about our respective illnesses. I think of Nietzsche, but don't mention it to her. It's better that way, because Inma is from the bedroom community of Móstoles, and when Nietzsche wrote about pain and women, he might well have been reflecting on the middle-class workingwomen who live on the outskirts of Madrid. Maybe I myself am one of those bourgeois ladies whom Nietzsche was talking about. But that's not really my social background, so I think, *Don't be so hard on yourself.* Meanwhile, I obsessively pick at the scab on my knee and enlarge the sore with the tip of my tongue. Inma and I decide we must get together. We promise.

Later, my friend Elvira sends me a depressing message on WhatsApp: "I can't believe they've closed the Café Comercial. So many memories. So many meetups there, so many beers . . . Marti, when you're back from your vacation, make sure to save a spot for us on your calendar to have dinner, before they shut down another pub on us." They've been closing down so many of them lately. We must be old—but not that old. Are we old? At the end of her message, Elvira adds the little yellow emoji that's blowing kisses. The mournful tone of Elvira's message is unusual. Every now and then I flip through WhatsApp on my phone, and I can see pictures of her children. I read her captions: "She's the brave one." "Just say no to sadness." She writes these after her daughter María has had heart surgery and after a ghastly series of family deaths. "Just say no to sadness," she writes. At first, I think she's silly. And then I understand why we've remained friends for almost thirty years. Today I open WhatsApp and Elvira has posted a new profile photo and status: "Happy Selfie." Elvira, even from afar and in her worst moments, makes me laugh.

So that's the sum total of my birthday: conversations about illnesses and shuttered bars. I have no idea if these topics arise normally among friends who grow older together or if I, somehow, am the one who magically invokes them.

MY CLAVICLE

I have a new GP, and she's sent me, electronically, a prescription for lorazepam. One hundred and fifty pills, two hundred thousand, a million. This easy access to pharmaceuticals makes me lose faith and interest. I give away some pills to my friends. So now I'm a trafficker and a *dealer*. I know the term *dealer* because I watch a ton of American movies and that's what they call them. "You can come back whenever you want." Yes, thank you, Doctor, I most definitely will want to come back. The shadow is still lurking there behind the door, it might emerge at any moment. The monster crouching at the back of the closet. The insects that may suddenly invade the entire house. The beast. Yes, I will come back very soon, because I've learned that stress is a very primitive response. Before we even walked upright, the intercostal spaces in our chest already contained a battery-powered warning light that flashed red when danger was imminent. We come unraveled when we think we can do it all but then realize we can't. Anthropology, naked apes, and Desmond Morris trample all over the sweet, civilized women who use opera glasses and are partial to morphine and epidurals, no matter how long or how thick the needle.

I start organizing my schedule for the next school year: classes, books, Bologna, the United States, Jerez de la Frontera, Córdoba, La Paz, Montevideo. And all the good things that will come. I'll return to that magnificent lifestyle that thrills me but also stresses me. I'll feel again that urge to do it all and the fear that I can't. I'll return to my awareness of privilege and of need. Be careful what you wish for in case your wishes come true. Things can go terribly wrong, like in W. W. Jacobs's classic horror story "The Monkey's Paw." I think of the long, bony fingers of the grieving mother clutching the magical monkey appendage that brings her deceased son back from the kingdom of the dead very much worse for wear.

Note to self: This book is distinctly culturalist. And full of *-ly* adverbs. I know what I'm doing.

MY CLAVICLE

Just at the moment when every cent I spend hurts, my parents, as a gift, invite us to join them on a cruise. My husband and I will enjoy the healthy, healing effects of a capitalist holiday. I think it's a wonderful idea.

As I read these lines, naturally I think of David Foster Wallace. And yet—*sarinagara*—a fundamental difference exists between his nautical adventure and mine: David was commissioned by a major magazine to go on a cruise and write about it. I suspect the idea that he wouldn't enjoy the experience, that he could not in any way accommodate what people expected of him, lodged in his mind even before setting out. He was an outstanding writer who wore a handkerchief tied around his head. Later he committed suicide, which is something I would never do no matter how many times some readers might ask why, or why not. It would be easy to do, of course. But throwing a tantrum about things that distress me does not equate to a desire to disappear. In fact, I don't want to disappear, and I love ghost stories and rational explanations for recordings of otherworldly spirits. My grandmother Rufi used to criticize my grandfather's obsessive health regimen. Every morning he'd splash exactly fifty handfuls of water on his face to wake up, then drink a glass of lukewarm water with lemon and eat a can of sardines in olive oil. My grandmother would say, "What? You think you'll cheat death that way?" She died of a brain tumor. I've always been grateful that I didn't inherit her beautiful, aquiline Spanish nose. She was a handsome woman in the symbolist style of a Romero de Torres painting.

So I go on the cruise. Because I feel like it. Of my own volition. There weren't any better offers for the summer anyway, and so I launch myself into the journey full of enthusiasm. Skepticism-free. I know from the start that I'm going to love some of the tacky excesses, like the smell of fried onions and junk food that was such a big part of my formative years at the beach in Benidorm and that I quickly sniff out at the ship's snack bars. That's another magnificent difference between myself and Wallace's "A Supposedly Fun Thing I'll Never Do Again": I'll be brief. Also, I can't be quite as clever, but I won't insist on recording every single conversation.

The economic crisis and the government's austerity policy and its fallout have made us old before our time. The belt tightening, benefits cuts, ridiculous government euphemisms, political profanities and angry outbursts, and personal income tax withholding and 21 percent VAT have all entered our bloodstream, like demonic bacteria, and are now, in fact, part of our platelet count and will cause the disease that, I swear to God, is going to kill us all.

I'm putting *me* back together again, top to bottom. I encase myself and all my jagged pieces in a cast. I am healing.

Here's what I remember about the cruise: "Papá, do they have boquerones in Stockholm?" A little boy peppers his father with questions as we all board the bus that takes us from the airport to a cruise ship that looks like the satellite where the earthlings in *WALL-E* get fat while floating in the pool sipping sugary drinks through a straw. "Ciao, ciao, ciao," shouts our guide who wears a moose head hat as he herds us like eager children during our daily excursions into the cities. The ship's staff—waiters, cooks, and security guards from Malaysia, Indonesia, or the Philippines—are all smiling. The cruise company appears to hire only very cheerful people and musical duos who at eight p.m. on the dot start to sing "Parole, parole," "Strangers in the Night," "Garota de Ipanema," "Te regalo una rosa." A selection of songs as international as the journey. The passengers are businessmen, bureaucrats, cops, retirees, the humble working-class folk who gussy up for dinner, wear purple, green, and silver reading glasses, tight russet-colored pants, ruffles, and beauty shop hair, and little girls who dress up as princesses and wander the ship from bow to stern: *"Guarda, la principessa!"* I start to feel an elitist nostalgia for Agatha Christie's cruise ships. On our ship, my fellow passengers talk too loudly and mock the staff, made up of people who can pretty much hold their own in four languages. A passenger alliance forms regardless of nationality. We are no longer Spaniards, Italians, Russians, Frenchmen, Brits, or Germans; we are simply a bunch of uncouth people who think we are above the service staff. We are the paying customers, and we whistle crassly for service and get irritated if the beleaguered but smiling waiter doesn't immediately understand what we say.

I watch all of this, and I am completely in my element.

Let's imagine the internal dialogue of these passengers, who somehow never seem to get drunk on their sugary cocktails.

We're here on this cruise to have fun, so we are gonna let loose and do it all. Start by dancing Zumba on Deck 11 at eleven o'clock: one foot in, one foot out, look down, turn around, lovin' it, up and down, and again, follow the rhythm of the instructor's ass, along with a hundred other people all in unison, all while knowing, of course, that we are not like them, that we are better than them, and that we are making fools of ourselves here just for now, and only because we want to enjoy this experience to the max, get our money's worth, relax, unburden ourselves, and blow away the haze of our daily lives by dancing the Zumba. Later we'll drink three orange-tinted cocktails with little umbrellas as we glance around the room and confirm to ourselves, yes, obviously, we are better than everyone else here.

We've made stops in Stockholm, Helsinki, Tallinn, and Saint Petersburg, and that was all fine. But Mom hasn't been feeling well the last few days. Her eyes itch and her joints ache. As her discomfort increases, mine fades. Has my mother's pain attenuated, umbilically, my own? Or are the healing effects of this capitalist holiday working? A change of scenery that finally gets me to stop tracking my tick.

On the flight back home, my parents hold hands during the landing. The flight attendant leans over them: Is it fear or love? She can't resist commenting: "I wish you two another fifty years of happiness."

My parents are very special. They're proud of their long and loving relationship. A sentimental feat. But the scrutiny of their small gesture of spontaneous intimacy, which in the past no one would have noticed, pains them. They laugh, but they are also offended. As if their life together, which is nobody else's business, had suddenly become a spectacle, abruptly making them feel old. Suddenly, instinctively, I understand everything, and lift my fingers to my Almásy's Bosphorus.

Marta Sanz is an award-winning novelist, poet, essayist, and scholar, and one of Spain's most celebrated contemporary writers. With a literary career spanning more than two decades, she has published fifteen novels and essay collections, including *Los mejores tiempos* (Debate, 2001), winner of the Ojo Crítico Prize for Fiction; *Animales domésticos* (Destino, 2003); and *Susana y los viejos* (Destino, 2006), which was a finalist for the 2006 Nadal Prize. Her recent works include *Farándula* (2015); *Círculo de lectores* (2016), winner of the Herralde Prize for the Novel; *Clavícula* (2017); and *Pequeñas mujeres rojas* (2020), a crime novel that appeals to collective memory, all published by Anagrama. Sanz holds a PhD in philology and is a critic for the *El País* literary supplement and for the magazine *Mercurio*. She was editor-in-chief of the cultural magazine *Ni hablar* and wrote for periodical publications like *ABC* and *Viento Sur*. Incredibly, while she has been published broadly in the Spanish-language world, *My Clavicle* marks her debut in English language translation. *My Clavicle* will be published simultaneously in the United Kingdom by Akoya Press.

Katie King is a journalist and literary translator with a PhD in Hispanic Studies. Her translations of Spanish poetry and prose have been published in *Words Without Borders, World Literature Today, Columbia Journal, Translation Review,* and *The Spanish Riveter* and in print anthologies published by Graywolf Press and Ecco Press. Her full-length book translations include *Someone Speaks Your Name* by Luis García Montero, director of Spain's Cervantes Institute, published by Swan Isle Press in January 2023, *One Year and Three Months*, also by García Montero, forthcoming from Vaso Roto in September 2025, and *My Clavicle*, by Spanish novelist Marta Sanz, forthcoming from Unnamed Press in July 2025. As a foreign correspondent and editor, Katie has lived and worked in London, New York, Madrid, Mexico City and Sao Paulo and traveled extensively in Spain and Latin America.